WHEN KINGS BEND

VI CARTER

WARNING

This book is a dark romance. This book contains scenes that may be triggering to some readers and should be read by those only 18 or older.

NEWSLETTER

Join my newsletter and never miss a new release or giveaway:

CHAPTER ONE

Diarmuid

As I step onto the dimly lit street, my gaze falls upon an unusual sight—a plethora of flowers left unguarded outside a small shop. The air is cool, and the quiet of the night surrounds me. Rows upon rows of petals, some wilting slightly at the edges, others vibrant as if plucked just moments ago. It's an odd contrast to the steel and concrete that tower over them. Perhaps an elderly shop owner had left them out, believing the good people wouldn't steal, that they might give a second thought to the shop's livelihood.

But I know better.

This world, with its fleeting moments of beauty, is nothing

but a façade. The tales of peaceful streets and good-hearted neighbors—they're mere fabrications sold to us by those in power. Governments say it's for economic success, when truly it's greed and religion's their salvation, when all they want to be are gods that walk the earth, all the while concealing the truth of their human nature. It's a nature I know all too well, having roamed these streets not as a guardian but as an example of what lurks in the shadows. Monsters are what they'd call us. Always taking, never giving back, leaving nothing but destruction in our wake.

The scent of the flowers hits me, overpowering in the stillness of the night. It's a smell I've never been fond of, one that many seem to cherish. They fill their homes with these vibrant colors and intoxicating scents, not realizing the irony. To me, it's the smell of death, of funerals—of endings.

The memories of those funerals linger in my mind, a mix of grief and unknowing accusations. Families wreathed in sorrow, their tears a testament to the void I'd carved into their lives. And there I stood among them, an unseen specter at the feast of their despair. It was a grim irony; the mourner and the cause of mourning intertwined, yet worlds apart.

The night deepens, drawing a veil over the city, and as I watch, the glass door across the street swings open, catching the glint of the streetlight. The sound of the church bell cuts through the silence, and my steps become cautious, deliberate. A group of jovial young men, spilling out from a pub and lost in their revelry, pays me no heed as I slip by, a mere ghost against the backdrop of their fun night out.

My target, the shop owner, remains oblivious to my presence. It's a pattern I've seen play out time and time again—the unawareness of those I follow, right until the very end. He's wrapped in a long coat to protect him against the chill of winter, his breath clouding the air in fleeting wisps. He locks up his store and continues down the street, passing more buildings until he slows down.

His path leads us to a quaint townhouse, its presence marked by a small brick walkway and a door painted a vivid purple. It's a splash of color in the gray concrete buildings we just passed. As he fumbles with his keys, a sudden apprehension takes hold, and he whirls around, his eyes searching the darkness for a threat he can feel but not see.

I remain still, a specter melded with the shadows, watching as he scans the night. There's a tension in him, a primal recognition of being hunted, yet without the sight of the predator. It's a dance as old as time—the prey senses danger, yet the hunter remains concealed, a breath away from revelation.

His gaze eventually moves on, dismissing the nagging feeling of being watched as nothing more than the night's trickery. The key turns in the lock, the door swings open, and I make my move.

As the shop owner turns his back to the night, I close the distance. There's a precision to the movement, a silence born of practice. The door is barely ajar as I push him inside, the sanctuary of his home no longer a safe haven but a stage for the night's final act. The click of the lock is a definitive sound, sealing our fates together in the confines of his world. Tomorrow his shop will not open.

I have no idea what this man has done, but he is on my kill list. With my arm firmly around his neck, he tries to look back at me, his mouth opening slightly like he's about to plead for his life. But that would do no good. Without giving him another second, I twist his neck, the break quick. His death is over in mere seconds. He slumps in my arms, and I carry him into his living room and lay him down on the floor. I stare down at the old man, wondering when I'll get tired of this. If I disobey, I will pay the price.

With a heavy exhale, I do what I do best. I spend the next few hours making his body disappear forever. He will become an unsolved murder, just like most of my victims are. Any cameras in the area will be wiped of my appearance. No trace of tonight's actions will be left.

Returning to my sanctuary, the grandeur of the wrought iron gates is a stark contrast to the dark deeds of the night. I find solace in the seamless integration of technology and tradition. The gates part at the command of my vehicle's signal, a silent welcome in the quiet of the night. In the rearview mirror, I watch them close, sealing me away from the world outside, from the city that pulses with life and death in equal measure.

Here, I am not the hunter nor the hunted; I am simply Diarmuid, master of this domain. Selene and Niamh are in the main living room, and when I arrive, both of them turn and take me in from my toes to the crown of my head. This is the norm for them. Checking me for wounds, like each time I leave, I might not return. Relief washes over both their faces, and it eases some of the tension in my shoulders.

"I'm going for a shower." I leave the statement open, letting them know they are welcome to join me. I very rarely take a shower alone anymore. Selene is the first to rise from the couch, the black silk nightgown clinging to her perfect body.

"We've just showered, but let me run the water for you." Her gratitude for how I keep her safe never ceases. I keep expecting them to defy my rules, but so far, they have been obedient. Grateful, even. Selene brushes her hand against mine as she walks past, but I circle my fingers around her wrist, stopping her in her tracks.

Pulling her into me, I place a soft kiss on her lips. "Thank you." She smiles, and I release her.

Niamh is still watching me. "How did work go?" she asks. I know she's wondering if I found Amira yet, but I haven't. Her mother is missing, too, and I'm wondering if her mother came to her senses and took off with Amira in tow. My men are still searching, but it's frustrating that there have been no sightings of her.

"It went according to plan." The shop owner's lifeless body assaults my thoughts, and I don't want to think about what I just did. I walk to Niamh and step to the back of the couch, reaching for her hand. I place a kiss there. "Work is boring; tell me about your day?" I say, pulling her up. She walks around to join me.

"Selene and I baked."

I smile as I walk. "I was wondering what the smell was."

She grins. "Liar; that was hours ago. I doubt the smell still lingers."

She's right; it doesn't. All I can smell is her sweet perfume.

The sound of the running water has Selene returning from the bathroom, and I start to take off my clothes. I'll have to burn them, so I place them in the trash chute. My maids know anything in there must be burned completely.

It's a pity; I liked the suit. Once I'm naked, Selene and Niamh don't leave but wait in the bedroom for me, and the thought of having two of my brides waiting makes me wash up quickly. We have grown close since everything has happened, in the most delicious ways.

When I re-enter the bedroom, the curtains are drawn, and the girls are sitting beside each other on the bed. I lean against the doorframe, just looking at them.

"You are both so beautiful," I say.

I hate that I must choose one, but for now, I can have both. I dry off and drop the towel—no need to redress—and walk to my brides. My cock is already hard. Selene licks her lips as she glances at my cock while Niamh rises. I touch Niamh's face and bring her mouth to mine. Selene's hands circle my cock, and it pulses as she strokes it with practiced motions.

Niamh's kisses are sweet, and I reach down, pulling the cord of her robe before pushing the garment off her shoulders. Beneath her small night dress, she wears no bra, and her breasts are perky and free. I grope one, and she groans into my mouth with pleasure.

Moist, wet lips circle my cock, and my head rolls back as Selene's lips make a path up and down my shaft.

She has gotten very good at pleasing me over the last few weeks. I've noticed such a shift in her attitude to me, as if saving them is something she will be forever grateful for. If I had thought that's what would make her bend sooner, I would have perhaps considered staging something.

But I don't have to. Niamh touches my cheek, directing my face back to hers. Her eyes shine with an innocence that I want to dirty.

I don't keep my kisses soft but grow greedy, slipping my tongue into her mouth. She groans, and when I pull away, I touch Selene on the crown of her head, and she releases my cock and rises. I want to see them kiss. It's something they have never done, but when I direct their faces together, they hesitate only for a moment.

"Kiss her," I instruct Niamh. She's more submissive and takes directions well. Niamh holds Selene's face, and they join lips. I stroke my cock as I watch them kiss for a few moments before moving behind Selene and removing her nightdress. She's also wearing only a small black nightdress.

"Touch her breasts," I whisper into Selene's ear before running my tongue along her earlobe. She does, and Niamh's eyes open. She looks directly at me over Selene's shoulder. Her dark eyes are a pool of black, swimming with lust.

"You like that?" I ask Niamh.

"Yes," her word is a mumble.

I reach around Selene and take one of Niamh's hands, placing it on Selene's breast before I let my hand trail down to Selene's stomach, my cock prodding into her ass. I continue my path all the way down until I touch the flesh of her thigh, before gripping her nightdress and pulling it up. I'm surprised she has no panties on.

"Were you expecting this?" I ask with a smile.

She breaks the kiss with Niamh and tries to turn, but I keep her in place. "Yes," she answers.

My fingers run across her mound before I find her clit and circle it. She leans into my chest, and Niamh continues to touch Selene's breasts, a look of fascination on her face.

"You can touch her, too," I say to Niamh.

She hesitates but only briefly. Selene doesn't object as Niamh's hand joins mine, her fingers trailing beside me before she pushes her finger inside Selene. Selene's gasp seems to excite Niamh as she pushes deeper.

When Niamh extracts her fingers, I can imagine how wet they are. I reach around with my free hand and take Niamh's hand, placing her wet fingers one at a time in my mouth. I suck off the moisture, and it tastes sweet. Niamh's mouth forms a small O as she watches me, and her innocent stare has my cock raging harder into Selene's backside, which pushes harder against me, telling me she's yearning for me to take her.

I spin Selene, and with two strides, she's at the foot of the bed, where I make her sit. "Lie back." She's ready to shuffle further up, but I grip her hips. Right, there is perfect. I stroke my cock a few times before I spread her legs, her pussy pink, wet perfection.

Niamh is at my side, looking down at Selene. She wets her lips, and I consider telling her to lick Selene's pussy, but my need to fuck her is too strong. I stroke my cock hard a few times before gripping Selene's legs and pulling her closer to me. Another inch, and she would fall off the bed if I weren't supporting her. My cock sits at her opening, and I turn to Niamh and watch her as I push all the way inside Selene.

"Kiss me," I say to Niamh, and she steps closer, her lips finding mine. The kiss is brief before I turn and focus on fucking Selene hard and fast. Her groans turn to moans, and her moans to shouts. She's loud when having sex, and it heightens my excitement as I fuck her hard. She tightens around me, and I'm surprised when she comes so fast. Her screams fill the room. My own orgasm is riding high, but I withdraw before I spill my seed and turn to Niamh.

"Your turn." I grin. "Take off your night dress."

Niamh has it over her head in a moment and positions herself, so she's bent over Selene, who's still reeling from coming. I push on her lower back, her face nearly all the way on Selene's pussy.

Selene raises her head and looks from me to Niamh.

"You can watch us come," I say to Selene before I push two fingers inside Niamh. She's soaking.

I remove my fingers and replace them with my cock. Niamh's hands grip the bedspread on either side of Selene's thighs. I push her face even closer to Selene's pussy. "Can you smell her cum?" I ask.

I push into Niamh in a slower rhythm, trying to prolong my own release, but I'm so close to coming. I can't hold back, especially when Niamh becomes bold and licks Selene's pussy. I'm fucking her hard before I explode inside her. I keep pumping until she raises her head, her shouts of pleasure driving me on.

"Come for me, sweet Niamh," I say.

On command, she cries out, and her wetness coats my cock. It's such a perfect mix. I slow my pace and place a kiss on her spine.

"Good girl." I'm sweating again. I always do when I have more than one woman to pleasure, but I enjoy having both of them in the bed with me.

Afterward, we shower and get into bed. With each bride lying on either side of me, I close my eyes with a contentment that's becoming all too familiar. But sleep is hard to find.

Staring at the ceiling, the soft breathing of my Niamh and Selene are the only sounds in the vastness of the room, but I am consumed by thoughts of Amira. The one who got away, the one I must reclaim.

CHAPTER TWO

Amira

The illusion of sunlight gently nudges me awake, a digital sunrise crafted by pixels rather than the warmth of a true dawn. For a moment, as my eyes flutter open, I allow myself the fantasy that I'm waking up to a real beach in Bali, not just the vivid imagery displayed across the flat screen that serves as my window to the outside world. The synthetic breeze rustles through the digital palm fronds, and the sound of waves, though recorded, brings a transient peace to my heart. I linger in bed, caught between the reality of my confinement and the escapism the screen offers.

It's a far cry from the reality of the world I was used to waking up in—fear of what the day would bring, fear of my mother, fear of being alone. Loneliness has always tried to suffocate me. From the death of two brothers to the disappearance of a third.

Michael. My mind wanders to him. If he was alive, what would he be doing now? What would he think about me? I push away the vulnerable thoughts. No one will think about me, so I must think about myself.

As I sit up, the room greets me with silence. Every piece of furniture, every fixture, speaks of a taste and wealth that I didn't have a say in but have become accustomed to. The professional touch is unmistakable, yet it's the personal touches I find myself missing the most. This isn't just a room; it's a gilded cage, beautiful but barred. I scoff at that thought as I climb out of bed; what personal touches could I possibly want? A bottle of vodka belonging to my mother hidden in some of my clothes or the bathroom closet?

No, this kind of impersonal I can get used to.

Yet, as I'm dressing for the day, it feels like I'm arming myself for battle. The clothes are another choice made for me, but I wear them like armor, a way to assert some control over my existence here. As I leave the bedroom, the guards stationed outside barely acknowledge me, their stoic faces a reminder of my status here. Not a guest, but not exactly a prisoner.

My hair, pulled back and secured, is the one thing I can control. It swings behind me, a silent testament to my resolve. The people I pass in the hallway step aside, their actions a mix of deference and fear. It's an isolation of sorts, a bubble of respect born from circumstance rather than genuine regard. The long, backless black silk dress sweeps along my feet, clad in gold sandals.

The doors I pass are like secrets, some silent and brooding, others whispering tales of what lies beyond. I've learned to navigate this place not with the sight of what's visible but with the sound of what's whispered. Each door represents a world, some in harmony with their inhabitants, others a silent battleground of wills.

The power I wield here is an odd one: respect without warmth, authority without freedom. As I walk, the weight of my situation sits heavily on my shoulders. Yet, there's a strength in me, a resolve that's been forged in the quiet moments of solitude and the loud din of expectations. I am Amira, defined not by my cage but by the spirit that refuses to be caged.

All of these rooms belong to Wolf's business. There are young women being trained for marriage and some simply for the sex trade.

I open the door to one of the sex trade rooms, knowing I will find Wolf there at work like he is most mornings. I don't close the door behind me but linger in the doorway. Wolf sits on a chair in the middle of the room, snapping his fingers at the woman giving him a blow job. He is instructing her, telling her how to do it *just* right.

"Relax your throat, and you will be able to take it all." His head is slung back in ecstasy. Since my stay here, I have heard him use this line so many times. Another is to *mind your teeth*. I step into the room and close the door behind me.

No one glances my way. All the women pleasing each other

are caught in capsules of pleasure. They're bubbles in an unstable world. Most of the women are naked. Hair color and eye color are their biggest differences, but their slim, close-to-perfect bodies are the one thing they have in common.

I step closer, and Wolf notices me. His lips stretch across his teeth, his head rising so he can take me in. I've become accustomed to his smiles, and like a fish on a hook, this one drags a smile out of me.

"You look gorgeous in black, a goddess," he compliments me.

I do agree with him. Black has always been a favorite of mine.

At our greeting, the woman stops, her mouth releasing Wolf's meaty cock, and straightaway his smile melts off his face. He grips her cheeks tightly. "Who told you to stop?" he barks.

The women's movements are jerky, almost frantic, as she takes Wolf's cock back in her mouth and continues sucking. He lets his head fall back again, and I weave between the other women in the room.

The air is thick with the smell of sweat and sex. Groans of pleasure hit me from every angle, and I find myself growing damp as I watch a woman buried in between another woman's legs. Her licks and sucks are noisy but not as brash as the groans from the woman she is pleasuring.

"Jesus, mind your teeth." Wolf barks again, and I can't help but return my attention to him. I exhale a loud breath and walk over, grabbing the woman's hair. I pull her head away from Wolf's cock, and she rises as I continue to pull her away.

"Watch and learn," I say.

Wolf raises a brow, and I grin at him before I gather my dress and sink to my knees. My hands run the length of his thighs before I grip his balls and give them a massage. I glance at the woman, making sure she is indeed watching; her scowl dissolves, but not before I see it. Anger whips at me. She has no respect; she must think we are equals. I stick out my tongue and flick it across the top of Wolf's swollen head. He groans, and when his hand touches my hand, I stop.

"You must have patience," I say.

His eyes darken, and as much as I want to show my power here, I know I truly have none when it comes to Wolf.

As if it is my decision, I wrap my lips around his cock, relax my throat, and widen my mouth, allowing his entire shaft to fill my mouth. I have learned to control my gag reflexes. I drag my mouth back up and tighten my lips against my teeth, making sure nothing nips his cock before I descend on his cock again.

His groans of pleasure make me excited and give me the confidence to keep going. My fingers keep touching his balls, running along the line that continues to his back passage.

"Oh, yes, Amira. Fuck."

Pride swells in my chest, and I'm sucking, licking, taking him all until air isn't even a thought. Making him come in front of the room filled with women is all I want to do. I want his seed to fill my mouth, drip down my chin.

My touches to his balls grow heavier, my nails run along the line, and the swell of his balls, the tightening of the skin, warns me of his oncoming end.

My saliva acts as a lubricant that makes noises with each stroke I make of his cock; he's jerking his hips, thrusting his cock into my mouth. But I'm aware he never touches my head, never forces me down on him.

He's almost wriggling in the chair when he can't seem to help himself; his final few thrusts are vicious, and warm fluid spills into my mouth, filling me up. I withdraw and hold all his semen before I release it onto the floor while watching the other woman.

She will pay for looking at me as less than her.

"Clean it up," I say, wiping Wolf's cum off my chin.

Her confusion draws her eyebrows close together.

"I said, clean it up."

She turns, and I know she's thinking of getting a towel.

I smile as I rise, letting my dress fall back into place.

"With your mouth."

She glances at Wolf, who's pulling up his trousers.

"You heard her." His words are barked, and my chest swells again.

The woman slowly descends to her knees. She glances up at me, and I'm close to pushing her face down if she doesn't obey me, but finally, she dips her face to the floor. Her tongue flicks out, and she licks up Wolf's cum.

"Swallow it, and don't leave as much as a drop," I order, and turn as Wolf slings an arm over my shoulder.

"A goddess you truly are." Wolf grins at me.

"Now, how do we get the rest of these in shape?" Wolf exhales as if the challenge ahead of us is huge.

Wolf approaches two women, keeping his arm around my shoulder. "These are the two most beautiful women I've ever trained," he says, looking down at two girls.

I glare at them. What makes them so special? Is it their sallow skin that has a shine off it, or how both of them have jet-black hair that flows across their bare backs? Their skin is blemish-free, and large brown eyes look up at us. I hate them already. He favors them over me.

"Maybe I will help them."

I shrug his arm off my shoulder. "No, let me," I say.

When I glance at Wolf, he grins. "Are you sure?"

I'm wondering if he is playing mind games with me, but as I glance down at the woman who seems to look at me with disapproval, I know I want to teach them a lesson.

"I'm sure," I respond.

Wolf places a quick kiss on my cheek. "Very well. Their pussies are too tight; I need them loosened up."

I hate how uncertain I feel now.

How do I do that? As if he senses my uncertainty, Wolf takes me by the hand and leads me to the far side of the room. He opens a large cupboard that's filled with sex toys. He withdraws a dildo that is not a fair representation of the male organs. It's too big.

"Maybe get one of them to use this on the other, and then they can swap." He hands me a large green dildo that flops from side to side. I touch it, and the texture is realistic if the size is not.

"I think I'll do it myself," I say, walking back to them.

They won't look at me again with disapproval.

Only fear by the time I'm done with them.

CHAPTER THREE

Selene

The air is alive with a gentle murmur as I approach my grandparents' house, a soft breeze weaving through the few leaves that cling to the branches of aging oaks. It's a familiar path, one I've walked countless times in my youth, but today, it feels different—like I'm crossing a threshold into a past I've long since left behind. The quaint, cobblestone path under my feet leads me to the porch.

I pause for a moment, letting the soothing symphony of the butterfly wind chime wash over me. It's a delicate sound, one that brings forth a surge of memories so intense it almost overwhelms me. My grandmother's wind chimes used to dance in the breeze by the dozens, creating melodies that filled the air with their vibrant, life-affirming songs. But that was before my grandfather declared he was one gust away from madness, leading to a household debate that ended with a compromise: one wind chime would remain. It had to be the butterfly one, the very chime I had chosen for my grandmother's birthday all those years ago, its significance now greater than ever.

Taking a deep breath, I lift my hand and knock on the door. The wait is brief. The door swings open, and there she is—my grandmother, her face lighting up with a joy that radiates warmth even before her arms are around me.

"Selene, my dear," she exclaims, her hands gently cupping my face as if to reassure herself that I am truly there. Her touch is tender, a balm to the soul, and when she kisses me on both cheeks, I'm enveloped in a sense of belonging that I've sorely missed.

Before I can fully embrace the comfort of her presence, another figure makes his way into the hallway. My grandfather, with his familiar shuffle and a smile that speaks volumes of the love he holds for his family, expresses his joy at seeing me in his own, understated way.

"Look at you, all grown up and traveling the world," he says, his voice carrying the weight of missed moments and pride in equal measure.

As we settle into the living room, the conversation naturally drifts to my travels. They're eager to hear about my adventures, the sights I've seen, and the people I've met along the way.

I find myself wrestling with a familiar, gnawing guilt that has become a constant companion on my journey. The stories I share with my grandparents, though true in essence, are draped in omission and half-truths. The world I paint for them, one of steady work and constant travel, is a facade that veils the reality of my freelance writing endeavors and the precarious life I've chosen since leaving my parents' house.

The warmth of their love and their genuine interest in my well-being make the deceit weigh even heavier on my heart. I've spun a tale of security and purpose, all the while knowing the danger that lurks just beneath the surface of my real life. After what happened to Rian, the risks of being anchored to one place became all too clear. Diarmuid invested in a new house for Niamh and me—a fortress veiled as a home, equipped with safeguards our old lives could never afford.

Sitting here, amidst the gentle clinking of the wind chime and the soft glow of the living room lamp, the reality of my choices hits me anew. These are my grandparents, who have given me nothing but love and support, and I've kept them in the dark. The thought of bringing any hint of danger to their doorstep is unbearable. I've convinced myself that this lie, this facade, is for the best.

"I've got a bit of work to catch up on before dinner," I announce, reluctantly pulling myself away from the comfort of the dining room chair. Their understanding nods do little to ease the tightness in my chest.

"We will let you get on with your work." My grandmother speaks first and plants a kiss on my forehead. My grandfather is more reserved at the thought of me leaving already. But I know lingering won't help, so I kiss him on the cheek and make my way to the apartment above the garage.

The garage, with its familiar scent of sawdust and motor oil, tightens my core. The door creaks open to reveal a darkness that feels almost suffocating, a stark contrast to the warmth of the house I've just left behind. With a flick of the switch, light floods the room, and the stark reality of my existence is laid bare before me.

The apartment looks like the physical manifestation of a deranged mind. Papers are strewn across every surface, and notes and photos are pinned haphazardly to the walls.

The room spins momentarily, a dizzying reminder of the double life I've been living. My fingers grip the edge of a table cluttered with papers and photographs as I steady myself against the sudden vertigo. This apartment, once a simple living space, has transformed into the command center of my obsession—an obsession born from the ashes of Rian's unfinished work. The evidence of my relentless pursuit is everywhere, in the photos and letters plastered across the walls, in the printouts and piles of material that claim every inch of space. Red string weaves a complex web between bits of evidence, a visual representation of the connections I'm painstakingly trying to piece together.

Diarmuid believes these visits to my grandparents are a respite, a return to normalcy in the chaotic aftermath of Rian's death. He doesn't know that instead of seeking solace, I've been chasing shadows, diving deeper into the rabbit hole Rian was consumed by. The guilt of my deception twinges at my conscience, but the drive to continue Rian's work, to expose the truth he died for, overshadows everything else.

As the room settles back into focus, I take a deep breath, trying to shake off the disorientation. It's been weeks since Rian was killed, weeks in which I've wrapped myself in layers of lies, presenting a facade to the world while my private life has been consumed by this investigation. Rian had been years ahead in his research, his knowledge far surpassing what I've managed to piece together so far.

Every time I return here, Rian's sacrifice looms large in this room, a silent echo in every scrap of paper and line of red string. He risked everything in his quest for the truth, paying the ultimate price for his bravery. The reality of his loss is a constant shadow, a weight that drives me forward even as it threatens to pull me under.

The images haunt me, unbidden and relentless—a spectral replay that jolts me awake in the small hours of the night, leaving my heart racing and my sheets cold with sweat. Rian, standing before me, his eyes wide with a mix of fear and determination, the moment before his life was snuffed out. It's a memory that clings to me, a shadow I can't shake, coloring every decision. I never thought someone's death would affect me so greatly. Watching someone brimful of love for life in one moment and dead in the next —gone in the snap of a neck—is an image I can't bear. It's there every time I close my eyes.

With a heavy sigh, I turn my attention back to the task at hand, my fingers moving almost of their own accord as they sift through the stack of papers before me. The Hand of the Kings, an enigma wrapped in rumors and whispers, has been the focus of my investigation—a group as elusive and shrouded in mystery as the Illuminati or the Freemasons. The deeper I delve, the more convoluted the trail becomes, with countless theories and conjectures clouding the truth.

Among the scattered documents, an article catches my eye, its headline bold and provocative: "The Hands of Kings: Alien Architects of Human Destiny?" According to the piece, this clandestine group wasn't just a power behind thrones but an otherworldly force, its origins tied to alien beings with a grand design for humanity. The theory states that these extraterrestrial architects seeded the Earth with human life, the Hand of the Kings serving as their intermediaries, selecting and guiding the leaders of these "herds" to fulfill an ancient agenda.

Skepticism wars with fascination as I read on. Other articles draw connections to biblical narratives, suggesting that hidden within sacred texts are references to this shadowy cult. Passages that have baffled scholars for centuries, the writers argue, are not mere parables but coded messages pointing to the influence of the Hand on human history.

But it's a claim by a conspiracy theorist that truly captures my imagination. This self-proclaimed expert asserts they've unraveled the core principles upon which the Hand operates, detailing edicts that dictate their actions. Edict IV resonates with a chilling clarity: "Kings are made to lead our world, but they must be guided. One Hand shall place the Kings in their places. One Hand should make Kings. One Hand should destroy Kings."

This cryptic phrase is one Rian had once uttered, his voice heavy with the gravity of his findings. It echoes in my mind as I pore over the notes spread out in front of me. "One Hand should make Kings. One Hand should destroy Kings." The implications of his belief is that there is a council above the Hand, above even Victor, who holds the reins of power.

If Rian believed in the existence of a higher council, then it was more than mere speculation; it was a lead worth following.

But it's the symbols associated with the group that present the most tantalizing mystery. Among the myriad documents, one phrase stands out, its letters seeming to pulsate with a significance I can't yet grasp: *luíonn an dorn ag Sí an Bhrú.* The language is unfamiliar, its meaning elusive, yet its repetition across several pieces of evidence suggests a significance that cannot be ignored. It's a clue, perhaps a key, to understanding the true nature of the Hand and the power it wields.

As the clock hands march forward, marking the passage of another hour, I know I need to return to my grandparents' home for dinner.

Reluctantly, I step away from my research, ensuring that every piece of evidence is secured, every document hidden away from prying eyes. The apartment above the garage, a sanctum of secrets and revelations, is locked up tight.

Dinner with my grandparents is a balm to the frayed edges of my nerves, a reminder of the life I'm fighting to protect. We engage in light conversation.

"I am completing all the crossword puzzles," Grandfather proclaims with joy.

My grandmother tuts. "That's because you spend days pouring over the same one. No more twenty-four hours with Selene working so much." She smiles at me.

Guilt churns again heavily in my stomach but I manage a smile. "Don't hold your breath; I will be back in the mornings to get the paper for myself," I joke.

My grandfather smiles as if the idea of me stealing the paper would bring him joy.

The meal ends, and it's as if my grandmother senses my unrest to leave. "I've been working on a new stew recipe. The next time you come, I'll have it ready."

I get up, using it as my cue to leave. "I look forward to it." I kiss them each on the forehead and head outside into the darkening evening. I don't look back as I promise myself I'll see them soon. Climbing into my car, I turn up the heat straightaway as I start to drive.

The city fades away in my rearview mirror as I navigate through the winding streets, the city's pulse giving way to the quiet of the outskirts where Diarmuid's new house stands like a fortress against the unknown. The rhythm of the music flowing through the car speakers is a temporary respite from the whirlwind of thoughts and theories about the symbols and their meanings. My fingers tap out an absentminded beat on the steering wheel as I try to mull over all the information I have gathered. It's frustrating when I keep coming up against a brick wall.

As the familiar outline of the property looms into view, the sight of Diarmuid waiting at the gate slices through the evening's calm with the precision of a knife. He's never waiting for me, and my first thought is to wonder if Niamh's okay or if something has happened. I freeze as I notice the gun raised in Diarmuid's hands. The abrupt sound of his gun firing into the air pulls a scream from me. The squeal of tires from behind, urgent and unexpected, sends a jolt of adrenaline surging through me. In the mirror, the car that must have been tailing me fades from sight.

"Are you okay?" Diarmuid asks as he gets into the passenger seat, still clinging to his gun. His expression is grim and alert. "I saw them following you," he says, his voice cutting through the racing of my heart.

How long had they been following me? The question pounds in my head with the force of a drumbeat. Did they know about the apartment, the research, the secrets I've been piecing together piece by precarious piece? The thought that my actions might have exposed us to unknown threats sends a chill down my spine, the shadow of Rian's fate a constant specter at the edge of my consciousness.

Diarmuid's hand on mine brings me back to the moment; his touch a grounding force. "We need to be more careful," he says. The strain and worry for my safety are visible in his eyes.

"Drive," Diarmuid commands as he turns and watches behind us like he's expecting the car to return. My hands tremble as I pass the gates, and in the rearview mirror, I watch them close, sealing us into our safe haven.

But I wonder how long we will truly be safe.

Who was following me?

CHAPTER FOUR

Diarmuid

I pull into the governor's sweeping drive. Winter is fast approaching, and with it, the holiday season. The mansion's windows are already adorned with red ribbons and electric candlesticks, casting a warm glow against the growing dusk.

I step out of the car, my breath visible in the cold air, and hand my keys to a valet. He nods, a silent promise to whisk my car away to the hidden groves that serve as a secluded parking area. The doorman greets me with a nod, offering to take my coat. But I refuse. I'm not here for pleasantries. I'm here for Victor.

"I need to speak to Victor," I announce, my voice firm.

"Victor isn't here," comes a voice from the shadowed side

of the entrance hall. Michael Reardon, Page to Victor, steps into the light, his presence commanding despite his lowly station within our ranks.

A Page is forever bound to serve, never to rise. Michael's lot in life is a cruel reminder of the rigid hierarchy that governs us. I stride past the doorman and the maid, who, rumor has it, knows more about poisons than most scholars.

Stopping before Michael, I size him up. The man's build is impressive, a solid frame that suggests both strength and endurance. In another life, he could have been a valuable asset to my family's more... physical enterprises. It's a shame, really, that his potential is wasted on being a glorified secretary.

The air in the mansion feels heavier as I recall the weight of the mistake Michael's father made—a blunder so colossal it threatened the very foundation of our order. A mistake that not only stains his family's name but chains three generations to a legacy of penance. Michael's children, innocent as they may be, are already marked by this shadow. The rules of our world are harsh, unforgiving. A reminder that failure carries a price far beyond personal downfall.

I notice the maid inching closer, her pretense of busyness fooling no one. I can't help but wonder what drives her—the loyalty to her poison master training or the simple human craving for gossip. Either way, she's too close for comfort.

"Let's walk, Michael," I suggest, my tone leaving no room for argument. My position within our ranks grants me certain privileges, one of them being the authority to command Michael, provided I don't overstep Victor's orders. Reluctantly, Michael falls into step beside me, his expression a mask of practiced neutrality.

We wander through the mansion, seeking a sliver of privacy. Yet, it seems as though every corner, every room, is staged with servants under the guise of their duties, ears pricked for any morsel of information they might overhear. It's like navigating a maze. A maze I know well.

By the time we've entered the fourth room, my patience frayed to its breaking point. Spotting a servant a little too conveniently positioned near the curtains, pretending to dust, I snap. With a swift motion fueled by frustration, I seize a chair and hurl it toward him. The chair sails through the air, crashing into the wall beside the startled man.

"Out! Now!" My voice booms through the mansion, echoing off the walls. The servants scatter. Finally, we're alone.

Turning to Michael, I lower my voice and prepare to speak, now that we're devoid of unwanted ears.

Michael beats me to it. "You cannot throw the property of the order around."

I pin him against the wall, my hand gripping his shirt, the fabric bunching under my fingers. His eyes widen with a mix of fear and the realization that I'm not here to chat.

"Where is your sister?" I demand, my voice low with a controlled calm that belies the storm raging within.

"I—I cannot involve myself—" Michael stammers, his voice barely above a whisper, but I'm not in the mood for excuses or deflections.

"WHERE IS YOUR SISTER?!" My shout echoes off the walls, a stark contrast to the hushed tones we'd maintained earlier.

Michael's resistance crumbles under the weight of my gaze, his defenses falling away as he confesses, "My King, I am sorry. I have been commanded by Victor to not have anything to do with my sister. That is why I could not attend the annual dinner. She cannot know that I am here."

I press on, knowing that Michael's position as Page to Victor grants him access to secrets and information that could be pivotal.

"You know all of Victor's secrets, right?" I probe, searching his face for any hint of deception or evasion.

Michael hesitates, the weight of his allegiance and the burden of his knowledge etched into the lines of his face. "One cannot begin to imagine the burden our Hand—" he starts, but I cut him off, my patience frayed to its breaking point.

"Stop simping, you piece of shit. You know his secrets." My words are sharp, a knife slicing through the air between us.

Michael's resolve hardens, a flicker of defiance in his eyes as he meets my gaze squarely. "Our Hand trusts me," he admits, a simple statement that reveals the depth of his loyalty and the extent of his involvement in the inner workings of our order.

I release him, stepping back.

Michael straightens his shirt. I should walk away, but I can't. I need to know where Amira is, and if anyone knows, it would be Victor. He has eyes and ears everywhere.

I spin and grip Michael again, forcing him against the wall.

"Then you know his…. special purpose for me?"

The revelation hits me like a physical blow, sending a wave of cold fury coursing through my veins.

"Then you know his…*special* purpose for me," I repeat, the words heavy with the gravity of our situation.

I can almost hear his heart pounding, a frantic rhythm against my clenched fists. Finally, he nods, a silent confirmation that sends a chill down my spine.

Michael's confirmation that Victor has a specific, dangerous purpose for me isn't surprising, but the knowledge that my Bride, my intended, is under the control of my own cousin is a betrayal I hadn't anticipated.

"Victor is a dangerous man; we both can agree on this. Michael, I am the man that dangerous men call," I say, the truth of my words hanging between us. It's a reminder of my role, my power, and the fear I can invoke.

His next words are cautious, laden with significance. "She is still under our control."

"How?" The question is a growl.

"She is with your cousin, sir." Michael's response is a grenade.

In a flash of rage, I slam him against the wall, the impact knocking photos to the floor, their frames shattering upon impact. "WHAT?! She is my Bride. She can't be sold!" The words are torn from me, a roar of anger and possession.

Michael, despite his predicament, retains a semblance of calm. "She isn't being trained, my King. Wolf has claimed her."

Wolf, who isn't even a Duke, took a Bride from a King.

Normally, there are consequences for this, but obviously, no one enforces those consequences.

The audacity of the move, the blatant disrespect, ignites a fire within me. Wolf, my cousin, has overstepped, challenged the very foundations of our order, our rules.

I need to get my cousin in line.

Releasing Michael, I step back.

"Michael," I say, my voice the calm before the storm, "thank you for your honesty. Stay out of my way."

As I leave him standing amidst the wreckage of our confrontation, I know what I must do. The game has changed; the stakes are higher than ever. Wolf has made his move; now it's my turn.

And in this game, I am the King. Wolf, my cousin, will soon learn that taking a Bride from a King is a move that comes with dire consequences.

The corridors of the mansion seem to echo with the weight of my resolve as I make my way out into the night.

CHAPTER FIVE

Niamh

The estate looms large and suffocating behind me as I make my decision. Diarmuid's command—that no one leaves without the proper escorts—echoes in my mind, a stark reminder of the cage I find myself in. Yet, the necessity of my journey demands discretion, something impossible to achieve with an entourage in tow.

The drivers, loyal to Diarmuid to a fault, are out of the question. They wouldn't dare defy his direct orders, not even for me. This leaves me with no choice but to rely on my own skills and cunning to escape unnoticed.

Years of training in the art of moving silently and gracefully, of becoming nearly invisible even in plain sight, now come to my aid. It's a slow, painstaking process, weaving through the house, avoiding the watchful eyes of Diarmuid's men stationed throughout the estate. Each step is measured, each breath controlled, until, at last, I find myself slipping through the gates and into the freedom of the night.

The city's public transportation system offers the anonymity I need. Boarding a bus to the Docklands, the center of Dublin, feels like stepping into another world. It's been ages since I last rode a bus. The memory of the last time I undertook such a journey lingers in the back of my mind—a reminder of Rian.

But I can't let the life I had slip away so easily, or my sister. It's her I'm doing all this for.

The bus slows down right outside the Bord Gais Energy Theatre. I slip off the bus and try to melt into the crowd. The air is filled with the anticipation of the evening's ballet. Each person is dressed to impress, with gowns and suits everywhere. My sweatshirt and jeans stand out among the crowd's finery.

I move inside the building, my stomach in knots as I remember Diarmuid's command.

The strict order for all to remain within the estate.

I approach the ticket box and steady myself, hoping my posture mimics someone who belongs here. "I am here for the O'Sullivan box," I declare, my voice steady, betraying none of the uncertainty that flickers beneath.

"Of course, the usher will take you there."

I'm surprised by how easy it is, and an usher appears on my

left. Although the usher's gaze lingers, perhaps a moment too long on my jeans and sweatshirt, he signals for me to follow.

"I would like to go backstage," I say after we have taken a few steps.

The moment the usher veers off the path I anticipated, my curiosity spikes, but I quell it. The O'Sullivans' connection to this place is not my concern—at least, not now. As the glitz and glamour of the theater's front house give way to the stark reality of its backstage, a wave of nostalgia washes over me. Despite the shift from opulence to practicality, there's something about the maze of bare floors, concrete walls, and the sight of pulleys and curtains overhead that feels like coming home. The scents here, a mixture of sweat, makeup, and the mustiness of costumes long used, are different from the world beyond the curtain, yet intimately familiar.

As I weave through the bustling backstage, ballerinas in various states of preparation catch my eye. Their movements are a flurry of grace and precision, each step, each stretch a testament to their dedication. I don't even know the name of the production, but the costumes speak volumes. Silver outfits adorned with stars, ethereal wisps of white tulle, and dark suits that render their wearers almost invisible against the shadows—all of it crafts a narrative I'm eager to unravel.

And then there's Ella.

She stands apart from the rest, not just in her role but in her very presence. Her dress, a cascade of white and pale blue, accented with scale-like makeup that traces a path up her arm to her face, is a vision of otherworldly elegance. I can't help but gasp at the sight of her, my sister, transformed into the epitome of what a ballerina embodies. In her, the grace and beauty of the art form are not just performed; they are lived…breathed. She is everything a ballerina is meant to be, and in this moment, she is everything to me.

Seeing Ella like this, so utterly transformed and yet so profoundly herself, fills me with a mixture of pride and sadness. Pride, for the woman she has become so quickly, and sadness, for the distance my journey has put between us, for the moments lost and the time it has taken to find my way back to her side.

I hesitate, just for a moment, before stepping forward. My presence here is a risk, a defiance of the orders that bind me, but the pull of family, of the bond between sisters, is too strong to ignore.

Pride radiates from me. When Ella's gaze meets mine, the transformation is instantaneous. The poised, enigmatic ballerina dissolves into the girl I grew up with—the sister who raided my closet and claimed the hot tub for hours on end. Her glide across the floor is a dance of a different kind. The moment she jumps into my arms, all the tension, the fear, and the distance melt away. We are simply sisters again.

Ella's grip is firm as she leads me behind the curtains to a secluded spot, a bubble of privacy in the midst of backstage chaos. The urgency and relief in her voice cut through me.

"Niamh, where have you been?!" Her words are a mix of reprimand and concern.

"I'm so sorry, Ella. I didn't mean to leave you," I respond.

"You should apologize! I have been so worried. Mama and Papa won't tell me anything. I thought something awful or shameful must have happened to you," she continues, her frustration and fear laid bare.

"I am fine. Taken care of. I have been worried about you," I assure her, trying to alleviate her fears, even as my own heart aches for the strain my disappearance has put on her.

Ella rolls her eyes, a gesture so quintessentially her, that I can't help but smile despite the seriousness of our conversation. "It's mostly just this. Mama is determined to make me a prima ballerina before I graduate."

Her admission brings a frown to my face. "Don't let her pressure you like that; it is rare for someone in high school to get that role," I caution her, aware of the immense pressure and expectations resting on her young shoulders.

"But she did it. I must do it, too," Ella says.

The bell's chime slices through our bubble of seclusion, a call signaling the start of the show. The hustle around us intensifies, a whirlwind of activity as performers and crew alike scramble into position. Ella's embrace, warm and grounding, becomes a sanctuary in the midst of chaos. I cling to her, the prospect of parting, even for a short while, a sharp pang in my heart. As she pulls away, I make a promise to her. "I'll check in again soon."

Reluctantly, I step back, allowing Ella to join the assembling groups. Her figure is a blend of grace and determination as she prepares to take the stage. The resolve in her posture, the focus in her eyes, speak volumes of the pressure she endures, the expectations she strives to meet. My heart swells with pride and concern in equal measure.

From my hidden vantage point behind the scenes, I watch as Ella begins her piece. The stage becomes her world, a realm where her hard work, her passion, and her talent converge into a display of breathtaking beauty.

Yet, as I witness her brilliance, a chilling realization dawns on me—the stakes of my own struggle, the consequences of failure. The Hands of Kings represents a threat not just to me but to Ella, to all I hold dear. In her performance, in the sheer force of her presence on stage, I see what must be protected at all costs.

Ella.

CHAPTER SIX

Diarmuid

I reach into my drawer and pull out the gun. It's heavier tonight, or maybe I'm just tired. It slips into the inner pocket of my jacket. I clip the last cufflink into place. I have an unavoidable outing, one I'd rather skip, but duty calls.

I'm just adjusting the jacket when the door creaks open. Selene. She doesn't knock anymore; none of us do. She steps inside, the light from the hallway casting a halo around her dark hair. She stops just a breath away, her hands reaching up to straighten the collar of my shirt. Her fingers are gentle.

These moments, these quiet, unspoken permissions we give one another, they've been happening more often. A touch here, a lingering glance there. It's as if the boundaries we once drew are slowly blurring into nothingness. I notice how my hands hesitate to pull away, how her breath catches slightly when I accidentally brush against her skin. I rarely shower alone these days, always joined by one or both of them.

Having my brides is a good distraction from the shit show my life has become lately.

Selene leans back against the dresser after ensuring every thread on my shirt sits perfectly. She fixes me with a look that's hard to read under the shadow of her lashes. Her hips push forward slightly, an unspoken invitation hanging between us.

"I worry about you," she whispers, her voice a mix of concern and something else, something deeper. "You don't have to do this alone, you know. We're here, we're always here."

I let out a breath I didn't realize I was holding. "I know," I reply, my voice rough like gravel. "It's just… complicated."

She nods, understanding flooding her features. "It always is. But remember, Diarmuid, complications don't make the man. The choices they make facing them do."

I smile, a small, grateful curve of my lips. "I'll remember that."

As I turn to leave, her hand catches mine, warm and reassuring. I have a little time. I turn to Selene and touch her face.

"Troublemaker." I say the nickname I had given her on our first meeting, but she doesn't smile.

I'm not sure what troubles her, but when I dip my head toward hers, her hands reach up and rest on my shoulders. She reaches up on the tip of her toes and presses a kiss to my lips that I accept.

Her kisses are feverish, and I slip my tongue into her mouth. Her breath is a mix of mint and caffeine.

I twirl her and direct her to the wall, my cock growing hard. I want to fuck her, but that is something I can enjoy on my return, so instead, I unbutton her trousers and allow my hand to slip down past her silky panties.

"What color are they?" I ask in between kisses.

"Red," she responds, knowing exactly what I am asking.

I grin into the kiss and let my tongue dance with hers. Fuck, I want her so badly. When my fingers sink between her folds and inside her, she's wet for me. The warmth flows across my fingers that I push inside.

She groans into the kiss, her hands trailing down my chest, their movements frantic, like she can't get enough of touching me.

I push a second finger in with ease and continue a slow rhythm as her core tightens around my fingers. Three fingers would be too much, so I continue with just two as I trail kisses along her jawline before stopping at her earlobe. I suck it in between my lips, nipping slightly. She gasps at the shock of pain, but the moan that follows tells me she likes it.

My access to her pussy is restricted. "Push down your trousers." She does within seconds and spreads her legs.

"That's it…good girl." I use my thumb to rub across her clit as I continue sucking and nipping her earlobe. Her chest is pushed against mine, and I run my hand along her side before cupping one breast through her top.

My fingers move faster in and out of her while my thumb works in quick circles across her clit.

"Oh, God, Yes, Diarmuid. That's it."

Her encouragement makes me move faster, and I slip a third finger inside her, widening her as far as she will allow.

"Oh. God." She groans.

I bite harder on her earlobe and squeeze her breast.

"Yes, yes." Her cries are loud, loud enough to attract attention, but my staff are used to their constant screams.

"I'm going to come," she cries out as her juices pour across my fingers. I kiss her ear as her body trembles with her release and trail more kisses down her jawline. I slowly extract my fingers before I release her breast and place a kiss on her forehead as she gasps for air.

"Good girl," I say.

She looks up at me, and I want nothing more than to have my own release, but I'm aware I need to leave.

I enter the bathroom. The cold water runs over my hands. I raise my head to look into the mirror, catching Selene's familiar outline behind me. Her reflection meets mine in the bathroom mirror.

An orgasm or two usually sends her on her way. Yet here she stands, an anomaly in her usual pattern of retreat.

"I would like to come with you today," she states, her voice cutting through the bathroom's serenity.

I pause, water dripping from my fingertips. It's an odd request. We have our shared evenings, but by day, we each retreat into our separate lives. Until now, neither Selene nor Niamh has shown any interest in what I do in the daylight hours.

"Why?" I ask, turning off the tap, reaching for a towel. The fabric scraps roughly against my skin as I dry my hands, turning to face her directly.

"I want to learn more about your role in all of this," she replies, her gaze steady, probing.

"You do understand that anything you see or learn must be kept a secret for the rest of your life?" My tone is stern, not out of irritation but of necessity.

"I understand," she assures me, her voice unwavering.

"I'm serious, pet," I emphasize, a flicker of concern etching my voice. "You could be killed for even whispering about it."

"It sounds like you are more scared than I am," she counters, a challenging tilt to her chin.

Selene's words linger in my mind like the aftertaste of strong liquor. It's not the first time she's been cavalier about the risks; her reckless bravery is both admirable and terrifying. Underneath that composed exterior, there's a tempest that she hides well— too well, sometimes. Add that to my growing list of concerns that seem to expand with each passing night.

I give her a nod, signaling that she should take a few minutes to prepare. While she disappears back into our room, I take the opportunity to walk down the hallway towards Niamh's door. My hand hovers before the wood, heavy with hesitation. The large bed in our room could easily accommodate all of us, even four, yet giving them separate spaces feels necessary, a small gesture toward maintaining some semblance of individuality.

Niamh hasn't emerged since the morning, and her self-imposed isolation isn't unusual. There's a quiet understanding between us that sometimes distance is needed—space to breathe, to be alone with one's thoughts without the intrusion of others. I let my hand fall away from the door, deciding not to disturb her sanctuary. She knows where to find us if she needs company or comfort.

Turning away from Niamh's door, I make my way back to the main part of the house.

When I return, Selene is ready, looking every bit the part of someone about to step into a world she doesn't yet understand.

"Ready?" I ask, my tone gentler than before. She nods, and together, we step out into the night. The air is cool and crisp. As we drive away, the house recedes into the background, a temporary sanctuary from the chaos of the outside world. My mind wanders back to Niamh, and I hope that her solitude provides her with the peace she seeks.

The pub is alive with the electric buzz of a Friday night, the air thick with the scent of ale and the distant cheer of football fans. The jukebox croons softly in the corner, ignored and overshadowed by the raucous shouts from the patrons watching the game.

Alan, behind the bar, spots us immediately. His nod is subtle, a silent acknowledgment. He doesn't miss a beat, pouring a pint for a waiting customer even as he gestures subtly toward the back. The unspoken communication is clear; everything will proceed as usual.

We weave through the crowd, the noise enveloping us like a second skin. Reaching the manager's office, I press a hidden latch, revealing the false wall. A brief glance at Selene shows her eyes wide with a mix of nerves and excitement. She's stepping into the underbelly of my world, and the weight of her trust in me feels both heavy and invigorating.

The secret room behind the office is just as I remember it from days spent overseeing its operations. Wooden crates, some marked with inconspicuous labels, are stacked neatly against the walls. The smell of gunmetal and wood polish is strong here, a stark contrast to the yeasty fragrance of the pub. Beer kegs connect to the bar above us, hissing softly with each use, a living part of the machinery that is my family's legacy.

"No one can say that you don't take me to nice places," Selene quips, her voice tinged with irony as she surveys the room.

I chuckle. "Only the best for you," I reply, guiding her to the metal table at the center. We take our seats, and the cold metal of the chairs is a stark reminder of the seriousness of this place.

Alan sends a quick text, his fingers moving deftly over his phone. Moments later, the door opens again, and more people file into the room. They're a mixture of familiar and new faces, each carrying the same determined, cautious look—the atmosphere shifts, thick with anticipation and the weight of unsaid things.

As the others stand, waiting for their turn to speak, I sense

Selene's slight unease. She leans in slightly, her voice low. "What happens now?"

"We listen, we plan, and if necessary, we act," I whisper back, keeping my eyes on the others in the room. "But remember, no matter what, stay quiet and observe."

The first to speak is Bob, one of my father's oldest friends and a seasoned veteran in our operations. He clears his throat, addressing the group with a measured tone. "As you all know, the situation in Venezuela has escalated. There's substantial civil unrest, and both sides are looking for an edge."

I nod slightly, aware of the opportunity it presents. It's a grim business, profiting from conflict, but hesitation or moral qualms don't have a place here. "We have shipments ready to move," I interject. "Payment has been secured from both factions. It's just a matter of logistics now."

Selene's gaze flicks to me, her eyes a mix of fascination and something darker, perhaps doubt or fear. I squeeze her hand under the table again, a silent message of reassurance.

Bob continues, shifting the topic. "In other news, the Americans have pulled out from another sector in Iraq. Left behind some heavy artillery, including tanks. We've secured them before ISIL could make a move."

Murmurs of approval ripple through the room. It's a significant acquisition, one that could bolster our standing significantly.

The room's mood shifts as Alan brings up a more somber subject. "There's something else we need to discuss. It's about Andrew O'Sullivan."

A collective breath seems to be held; Andrew's recent disappearance has been a shadow over all of us. "Rumors are that he was taken out by a hit. An organized one," Alan continues, his face grim. "If that's true, whoever did it might not be finished with us yet."

Selene stiffens beside me, her earlier excitement giving way to the stark reality of our lives. The danger isn't just a story or a thrilling secret; it's real and palpable.

"We need to tighten security," I say, my voice firm. "Everyone needs to be more cautious. We don't know who we're dealing with, but we have to assume they're serious."

Nods of agreement meet my statement. The rules of engagement are clear: stay alert, trust cautiously, and protect your own.

"They are," Alan interjects and glances around the room at all the men. "Oisin Cormick has been missing for several weeks. The old man was retired from the game, and people are starting to worry that he was a victim of a revenge hit."

I knew the disappearance of Oisin would finally be brought to the table, so I was prepared to give nothing away, but I used this opportunity to watch Selene's face during this particular part of the meeting; I wanted to see if she was capable of hiding the truth.

She doesn't flinch. She passes.

The meeting comes to a close, and I'm the first to rise. Selene follows suit, refraining from asking any questions until we are out of the pub and back in the car.

She gnaws on her bottom lip, the wheels spinning in her mind.

We drive for a few miles before she speaks.

"What happens when everyone finds out about Oisin?"

"They won't," I reassure her.

"But if they did?"

I glance at her before refocusing on the road.

"The Hands Kings would have my head."

She takes in a large lungful of air.

I reach across and place my hand on her leg.

"They won't, Selene. I'm too good at what I do," I say and hope I'm right. I was sloppy with Andrew and Oisin, two kills that could cost me so much, but once I find out who set me up with Andrew's death, I'll pin Oisin's death on them, too.

I'll kill two birds with one stone.

"I know what happened to Oisin Cormick," she states, her voice steady yet carrying a hint of trepidation. She pauses, as if measuring the impact of her words before continuing, "I just have to ask; do you know what happened to your uncle?"

Her question gives me pause. She already knows I killed my uncle, so why is she asking me again? I wonder if she is testing me.

I don't answer but give her a long look, trying to gauge what game she is playing.

Selene doesn't say another word for the rest of the drive.

I know when I told them the truth it was shocking, but the sooner my Brides knew, the better.

After all, if I overplayed my hand, they would suffer just as much as I did.

CHAPTER SEVEN

Selene

I lean against the frame of Niamh's door, watching her stretch on the floor, utterly absorbed in her routine. Her limbs move with a grace that seems almost effortless, a stark contrast to the clumsy attempts I remember from my brief stints in sports. My parents never minded what I picked up or dropped as long as I was doing something. Hockey, track, dance—you name it, I've probably tried it for a season.

Niamh is different. She's like a piece sculpted with a purpose, her whole life molded around the perfection of ballet and the rigors of competitive swimming. There's something almost enviable about her dedication, her entire being honed for performance and precision.

She notices me lingering in the doorway and pauses, mid-stretch, her gaze lifting to meet mine. "Selene? Come in," she calls out, her voice light but curious.

I push off from the doorframe and close the door softly behind me, my steps cautious. We both know that walls have ears, especially in places like this. Diarmuid might be generous, but my trust has been hard-won and easily lost. "I was wondering if you'd like to go grab a coffee with me," I venture, keeping my voice low.

"Coffee?" Niamh frowns slightly, sitting up to face me fully. "What for?"

I scan the room as subtly as I can. It looks normal—sparse, tidy, nothing out of the ordinary. No hidden cameras in sight, but then, the best ones never are visible. I perch on the edge of the bed, watching as Niamh reaches back to stretch her leg, her hand brushing her heel. "I thought that we should meet someone today," I say, trying to gauge her reaction.

"Meet who?" Her brow creases, and she pulls her leg in, resting now. Her body tenses slightly, the casual ease replaced by guarded curiosity.

"Just a friend," I say quickly, "someone who might help us understand a bit more about… well, about everything." My mind races as I watch her, trying to read her thoughts. Has she grown too comfortable under Diarmuid's protection, or does she, too, feel the prickle of doubt when the lights go out?

Niamh looks at me, her eyes narrowing slightly, not with suspicion, but calculation. "This isn't just about coffee, is it, Selene?" she asks, her voice steady but low. She hesitates, her expression guarded. "I feel like I've met enough people lately, thanks."

I press, knowing how much rides on today. "This person is a relation of our mutual friend." The phrase 'mutual friend' hangs between us, a code that has come to mean only one person: Sofia Hughes.

At that, Niamh straightens, the reluctance in her posture melting away, replaced by a sharp spark of interest. "Okay, let's go then," she says, her tone shifting, infused with a new energy. This meeting, after all, has been weeks in the making.

Ever since the loss of the crucial evidence from Rian's apartment, I'd been scrambling to piece together what could be salvaged. Rian had years on me, his collection extensive and meticulous, while I was playing catch-up in a game I barely understood. But Sofia Hughes' name was a beacon that remained clear in our minds, unerased and indelible.

Diarmuid had arranged everything—escorts, transportation, the works. I'd played my part, too, claiming a desperate need for normalcy, a break from the cloistered existence we'd been living. As if anything about my life could ever be considered normal.

We're picked up in a sleek black Audi, the anonymity of the vehicle doing nothing to ease the tight coil of apprehension in my gut. With two men in the front—probably more of Diarmuid's people—it isn't safe to speak openly. I can't just tell Niamh everything, not with potential ears in the driver's and passenger's seats. So, I pull out my phone, open the notepad app, and start typing. Niamh watches, her eyes flicking to my screen as I hold it up for her to read.

Can't talk here. Everything might be monitored.

She nods slightly, understanding, and takes the phone from my hand to type her response. We continue this silent conversation, our words hidden in plain sight, never sending anything that could be intercepted. After all, Diarmuid had provided these phones, and neither of us is naive enough to believe our communications are not being monitored.

Do you trust this contact? Her brow furrows as she hands the phone back to me.

As much as we can trust anyone now. It's our best shot at getting answers.

She reads the message, her lips pressing into a thin line, and then nods, handing the phone back to me.

The car hums softly beneath us, the cityscape blurring by as Selene and I maintain our dual conversations—one audible, light, and seemingly inconsequential, the other silent, heavy with the weight of our true intentions.

"Have you found anything nice to wear?" I ask aloud, ensuring my voice carries easily to the front seats. "The color restrictions are driving me crazy."

On my phone, I type swiftly, my fingers barely keeping pace with my racing thoughts.

I tracked down Sofia Hughes' sister. Her name is Maura. That is who we are meeting today.

Niamh laughs, a little too brightly, but it serves its purpose. "I am having the same problem! No reds, oranges, greens, purples… during autumn. This is the season of bright colors."

She then glances at the phone, her fingers tapping out a response.

Her sister?! How did you get her to meet with us? What did you tell her?

"I am leaning toward a dark blue with golden accents. What do you think?" I continue aloud, describing an outfit that I haven't even picked out yet. Privately, on the phone, I reply, *I told her that we may have information about what happened to her sister.*

Niamh's face flickers with a mix of emotions—revulsion, fear, anticipation—as she reads my message. Out loud, she keeps up her end of the trivial chatter. "That sounds lovely, very elegant. Maybe I should go with something similar... keep it classy, right?"

Her fingers hesitate before she types back. *This is risky, Selene. If Maura knows anything... or suspects...*

I nod, understanding her concerns, both spoken and unspoken. "Absolutely, we should coordinate. Can't have us clashing; it would be the talk of the evening," I say, chuckling as if we were discussing nothing more serious than fashion choices.

In our digital whispers, I add, *We need answers, Niamh. We're flying blind otherwise.* I pause, then decide to share more, hoping it will solidify her resolve. *And there's more. No one mentioned that the missing Sofia Hughes had been found or how. But they reported heavily on the body found buried under where she was last seen.*

Niamh reads the message, her expression darkening for a

moment before she schools her features into neutrality. Out loud, she says, "Maybe a touch of gold in the accessories then? Could brighten up the evening."

Silently, she hands the phone back to me after typing, *We're in too deep to back out now. Let's see this through.*

As we exchange our phones back and forth, our spoken words light and frothy, our written ones dense with the gravity of our real predicament, the car turns smoothly onto a broader avenue leading us away from the heart of the city. Toward answers, toward danger—toward Maura.

Our visit to the morgue had been grim and unyielding. The official report branded Sofia's death a suicide, a neat, convenient label to close the case. Yet, the assistant at the morgue, her face pale and her voice barely above a whisper, had confided in us that she didn't agree with the official narrative. "Things don't add up," she had said, her eyes darting nervously around the cold, sterile room. That conversation echoed in my mind.

Aside from this, all we really knew was that Sofia had been employed in some administrative capacity for the national government—a position that might have given her access to sensitive information, perhaps enough to put her in danger. It seemed likely that Maura was aware of her sister's governmental role, but whether she knew the darker undercurrents of Sofia's fate was another matter entirely. The question loomed heavy between Niamh and me: were we the ones destined to reveal the truth to Maura about how her sister really died?

Lost in these thoughts, I gaze out the window. The Audi slows as we approach our destination, the quaint facade of the coffee shop coming into view. It's nestled on the corner of a street paved with traditional cobblestones, picturesque and bustling on this bright autumn day. Patrons are already gathered outside, enjoying the crisp air and spiced coffee aromas that mingle with the fallen leaves. I squint, scanning the crowd for any sign of Maura.

A gentle bump against my arm has me turning. Niamh offers her phone to me. On the screen is her latest message,

Why are we so obsessed with this?

It's a good question—one that haunts me in the quiet hours of the night when the world seems to stand still except for my thoughts. I quickly type back. *We can't do anything for ourselves; maybe we can do something for her.*

We park a street over from the coffee shop. Our escorts, a pair of hired grunts, amble behind us with a disinterested gait. They're typical in their detachment, barely acknowledging our existence beyond their duty to follow. Thankfully, they keep their distance, choosing to lean against a nearby wall, giving us a semblance of freedom to get our coffees in peace.

With a cup of bitter brew warming my hands, I scan the crowd. It doesn't take long to spot Maura. I know her only from photos—photos that included Sofia, always vibrant and alive, a stark contrast to the stillness of her in death. Seeing Maura in person jars me. She hasn't noticed us yet, allowing me a moment to study her from afar. There's something unexpectedly ordinary about her as she sits there sipping her coffee, lost in thought.

Maura's beauty strikes me immediately as we approach

her table. There's a grace to her features that's undeniable—a testament to the genetic jackpot her family seems to have hit. Her lips are naturally plump, curving elegantly over a chin that tapers to a gentle, sleek jawline. Her eyelashes are enviably thick, curling naturally at the edges of her soft, melancholic eyes.

In the photos I had seen of Sofia, she had always appeared either professional or radiantly happy. The contrast with Maura, sitting before me, is stark. Her face seems drained of that familial joy, shadowed by dark circles under her eyes that tell of sleepless nights and a grief that clings tightly. Those eyes… they look out into the distance but seem to see nothing. They remind me painfully of my own reflection on the worst days after finding out why my parents had me, for one thing—for no other reason than to marry me off to gain power.

With a gentle approach, I greet her softly, "Maura?" My voice is cautious, unwilling to startle her.

She doesn't jump; there's no sudden movement, no flicker of surprise. It's as if it takes her a few moments for her mind to wander back from its distant thoughts, to realize someone is actually speaking to her. The sadness of it grips my chest with a tight fist.

"Hi, Maura. I'm Selene, and this is Niamh," I introduce us, stepping closer but maintaining a respectful distance. I want to give her space, physically and emotionally, to adjust to our presence.

Maura gives a slow, almost imperceptible nod. Her acknowledgment is subdued, her expression unreadable as she assesses us, perhaps trying to piece together why we're here. Her gaze shifts between Niamh and me, a flicker of curiosity briefly cutting through the fog of her sorrow.

"May we sit?" I ask.

She nods. I glance at Niamh, who pulls out a chair, and I follow suit.

As we settle into the slightly uncomfortable metal chairs at Maura's table, I lean forward, clasping my hands together on the tabletop. I glance at Niamh, who looks back at me with a slight unease. "Maura, Niamh and I are sisters," I begin, ignoring the way Niamh stiffens beside me. My words spill out rapidly, a deliberate ploy to keep Maura from noticing Niamh's reaction. "We lost our other sister, Amira, recently. Your sister's story... it resonated with us."

Maura's expression softens, her eyes meeting mine with a depth of understanding that only comes from shared pain. "I'm sorry for your loss," she murmurs. "Only those who've been through it can really understand."

Her words slice through me, and I fight to keep my composure, to not let the guilt of our fabricated story show. I nod, briefly closing my eyes. "Thank you, Maura. It means a lot hearing that from you."

She shifts in her seat, her gaze dropping before she looks up again. "Sofia and I were very close, as close as sisters can be," she says, her voice thick with nostalgia. "She was full of dreams, wanting to see the world, make a difference. She took an internship in the office of Tyrone Lynch."

At the mention of the name, a jolt of recognition. Tyrone

Lynch isn't just any name—it's a name that rings with authority and power across Ireland. "Tyrone Lynch," I echo, "the former Minister of Justice." He is now our Taoiseach, selected by the President.

"Yes, and I think his office knows more than they're letting on about what happened to her," Maura continues, her voice hardening with a mix of suspicion and determination.

Maura's glance flickers to me, probing. "Do you know anything about the case?" she asks, her voice barely above a whisper.

I shake my head, my face mirroring her solemnity. "Only what's been public, nothing more."

As she hears this, tears well up in Maura's eyes, and she turns her head away, looking back toward the distance she had been staring into when we first arrived. The haunted look in her eyes is painful to witness. It's a look that speaks of broken dreams and unresolved questions—a look that tells me she's far from finding the peace she deserves.

Maura's voice trembles as she gestures to the bustling street outside the café window. "This is the last place I saw her."

My heart sinks as I listen, the heaviness of her loss palpable in the air. "I'm so sorry. I didn't realize," I reply, my voice soft, filled with genuine regret.

"I had not seen her for months," Maura continues, her gaze lost in the past. "Most of the family had written her off, but I knew she was off following her dream. We had a coffee, and I ended the visit... I wanted to get to a store before it closed. So stupid. When I look back—you just don't know when these things will happen."

Niamh, who had been quietly absorbing the weight of Maura's words, interjects gently, "There is no way you could have known."

Maura nods, tears brimming in her eyes. "She crossed the street right there, waved at me, and disappeared from my life. I never saw her again." She pauses, her voice breaking. "I keep looking, expecting her to pop back into my life. But she won't."

Turning to me, Maura's eyes plead for answers, for any shred of hope. "Please, do you know anything?"

I'm torn, the weight of Maura's gaze pressing down on me. I know that someone powerful was involved in Sofia's disappearance, someone who could change the course of our investigation and potentially our lives. Woman-to-woman, Maura deserves to know the truth, deserves any piece of peace that could come from it. But then, the image of Rian flashes through my mind, and the danger of drawing Maura deeper into this murky world holds me back.

"I'm sorry," I say, the words tasting bitter on my tongue. "I know as much as you know."

As Maura's face falls, the ease with which the lie slips out disturbs me. I'm becoming too accustomed to lying. The realization sits uncomfortably within me, a stark reminder of how far we've strayed from the straightforward paths of our past lives.

CHAPTER EIGHT

Amira

The nearly empty room amplifies each sound with terrifying clarity. Echoes of screams fill the space, mingling with scratching that mimics the scurrying of rats. It's damp, dark, and desolate—a stark contrast to the other rooms in the building, which hold remnants of normalcy and light.

From outside the cage, I watch. My mother is trapped inside, her body writhing as the LSD coursing through her veins conjures monsters from the shadows. Casually, I run a bat along the cold metal bars, the clinking sound of wood on metal sending shivers of fear through my mother with each contact.

I haven't laid a hand on her—I don't need to. The drugs are

doing more than I ever could, more than I ever did. All those years of abuse, every moment my mother had made me feel small and scared; it's all being repaid now, tenfold.

My mother's screams eventually taper off into whimpers. Eyes wide, she scans the room fearfully, every shadow a demon, every sound a threat. With a calculated swing, I hit the side of the cage sharply. The metal clangs loudly, and my mother's screams shatter the brief silence again.

The act, while passive in its violence, is brutal in its intention. I stand there, a figure of calm vengeance, as each scream pierces the stale air of the room. I watch with a cold detachment, the bat hanging loosely in my hand. The echoes of my mother's terror are a chilling reminder of the years of torment endured, now returned in a twisted form of justice.

Her screams continue, piercing the fog in my mind. I don't linger but drop the bat and leave the room.

Wolf waits for me in the hallway, coolly leaning against the wall as if I'm coming from a shower and not a torture session with my own mother.

Wolf pushes off the wall. "You know, I could add some ecstasy to that cocktail. It would be hilarious to watch her fuck that bat."

"I'll keep that in mind," I mutter, the words hollow between us. My eyes flick away from Wolf's amused gaze, focusing instead on the cold, unwelcoming floor. Deep down, a tangled mess of emotions begins to surface. Despite the horrors my mother inflicted upon me, a tsunami of pity forms in my heart. It's unsettling, this softening. For years, I've cloaked myself in a guise of unrelenting cruelty to mask my own vulnerabilities. But now, as the tables have turned, the necessity of this cruelty seems... pointless.

Wolf, however, embodies a different breed of darkness. He revels in the suffering of others, his eyes sparkling with a disturbing glee at the prospect of pain, irrespective of any personal connection—or the lack thereof. It's chilling, his detachment, his ease in the face of others' agony.

He suddenly produces a long jewelry box, extending it toward me with an unsettling smile. I hesitate, my instincts screaming caution. Trusting anyone linked to the cult is a gamble I'm all too familiar with. "Take it," he commands, his voice a mixture of impatience and authority.

With a resigned breath, I accept the box, the polished surface cool to the touch against my skin. Slowly, I lift the lid to reveal a necklace, its emerald pendant glinting ominously under the harsh lighting. The stone's deep green is mesmerizing, yet the weight of accepting such a gift feels heavier than the jewel itself.

"Thank you," I stammer, the words catching awkwardly in my throat.

Wolf's eyes light up, not with the stable flame of power, but with a wild, uncontrollable inferno—a fire that threatens to consume both bearer and beholder. "Emerald, the stone of rebirth," he declares.

"It's beautiful, Wolf," I say, my voice steady as I run my fingers over the cool, smooth surface of the emerald.

Wolf's eyes hold mine, and for a moment, his voice softens, almost tender. "You have a chance for a new life, Amira. With me.

Fuck anyone who comes near us." His words start as a promise, a whisper of new beginnings and a life far removed from the chaos of our pasts.

But as he continues, his tone shifts. It hardens, his speech accelerating, growing angrier and more unhinged. I tense, sensing the dangerous swirl of emotions building within him. This isn't just passion; it's volatility.

"I mean, fuck, we deserve that, don't we? Fuck, look at your family. Your brother, Dominic, forced to take the shittiest jobs for my family just to get fucking blown away by the Garda," he rants, his voice rising.

"Yes, Wolf. It wasn't fair. I think we should—" I try to interject, to steer the conversation back to calmer waters, but he cuts me off.

"—then your mum goes fucking nuts. This makes your other brother—Kevin, right? He tries to self-medicate and ends up in a fucking body bag."

His words, meant to stoke a shared outrage, only leave me feeling hollow. "None of that matters, Wolf. I have you now," I reply, attempting to anchor him back in the present, away from the ghosts of our past grievances.

But Wolf's eyes blaze with an untamed fury, unappeased. "WHY?! Because your da' fucked up. That's it. Your da' fucks up, and your brothers are gone, and you get pawned off to Diarmuid fucking O'Sullivan."

Wolf's movements are sudden and catch me off guard. With anger in his gaze that I've never witnessed before, his hand circles my throat, and my back connects with the wall. The jewelry box falls to the floor.

"Any sin can be forgiven, except for the sin of abandonment. The abandonment of the order will be felt by the wrongdoer for three generations. Edict fucking two! Do you know who left the order?" Wolf's words roar into my face.

Even if I wanted to respond, I couldn't, as he squeezes his hand around my throat, taking my breath away. He isn't drunk. He isn't high. No, it's worse. This is pure, uncontrolled rage.

"Diarmuid's father. Richard O'Sullivan, met his wife and thought he could make it on his own. He left the order, left the mafia, left everything. When he fucking struck out, he came crawling back. *ALL* was forgiven."

I hit his hand, but he doesn't release me. I can barely whisper his name to try and get him to let me go. I'm struggling for air. He's choking me. Darkness forms in the corners of my vision. His face draws nearer to me, his teeth closer to my ear.

"Forgiven like my father's killer." Wolf's words barely register, but he releases my neck, and I don't have a chance to suck in air before he forces his mouth onto mine.

His hands run down my body, the touch rough and frightening. I push against his chest, but it's like pushing against a brick wall. His tongue slips into my mouth, and I clamp my lips together, restricting his access.

His hand lodges at my throat again.

"Open your mouth!" The madness in his eyes should have me obeying. I should obey. Instead, I slam my hands against his chest.

I'm shocked when he releases me, but his laughter chases away any relief I feel. A flood of fear chokes me worse than his hands did. He lunges, and the tear of fabric makes me try to piece my dress back together. He's on top of me again; the force of his body against mine sends me sailing into the wall. The sound is muffled, and I blink to clear my vision.

His trousers are down, his intention clear. My hand strikes his face, and his laughter shatters the bubble of silence. Before I can react, his hand lands heavily on my face. I hit the floor, smashing heavily on my stomach. Not for long, though. Wolf swings me around to face him as he climbs on top of me.

"Get off me!" I roar and spit at him. My saliva lands on my own chin, not deterring him at all.

"You are mine," he says, wedging my legs apart.

I'm trying to get away, clawing at the floor either side of me, my nails straining—

My body jerks as he slams himself into me. Shock has me limp as he thrusts with a viciousness I've never seen or felt before. I've been beaten, insulted, but this—

"Noooo." I claw at his face. He grabs my wrists and slams them on the floor as he continues his animalistic thrusts.

Tears flood my sight, and I'm screaming. Screaming for help. The maids move in the distance, but they quickly turn away.

"No, no, help me," I sob, my throat aching, but it's nothing like what's happening on top of me. I buck only to have him slam my wrists into the floor again, screaming as my bones protest against the abuse.

"Please!" The word trembles and spills from my lips.

He won't stop.

"Please." My mind starts to shut down, each thrust rocking my body with pain, pain that is so much deeper than anything I've experienced. I don't know when he stops, but I'm still sobbing, repeating *please* over and over again.

"Get up." He runs his hand across his nose before pulling up his trousers.

I rise. I don't know how, but I try to pull the shreds of my dress together, but not before I notice blood staining the inside of my thighs. A sob fills the hall, and I find myself on my knees.

"You are mine," he says. His voice is calm.

"You …" I swallow the sob. He turns away and buttons up his pants. He raped me.

Salty tears fill my mouth, and I try to stand again. My hands wrap around my abdomen like they can stop the pain. The humiliation.

Suddenly, the jewelry box is pushed into my face.

"Put it on," Wolf commands.

He keeps the box outstretched. I reach out and take the necklace. Bile rises in my throat. Wolf walks behind me and takes the necklace from my hand. My tears stop falling as he places the necklace around my neck. When he steps back into view, he gives me one of his charming smiles.

"Beautiful." He touches the necklace before touching my cheek. "We need to prepare for the event tonight at the Hands of Kings."

I nod, and he presses a kiss to my cheek before he walks away. I stand and watch him go. I'm pathetic, but I don't want him to leave me. I have no one else.

"What are you crying for?" My mother's words follow me down the hall. *"More crocodile tears; you are disgusting."*

I swallow the pain and bury it with the rest of the hurt. I need to be strong.

A maid who's walking past stops. "Would you like a new shirt?"

It's one of the maids who ran away while Wolf raped me.

My hand connects with her face, the slap loud in the empty corridor. She stumbles and falls to the floor.

I stand over her. "I will dress however I damn well please."

CHAPTER NINE

Niamh

I stand in the foyer, hands gliding over the tight, soft fabric of my sweeping ballgown. The texture under my fingers is luxurious, a testament to the skill of the seamstress Selene and I entrusted with our attire for tonight's moon-themed event. I can't help but grimace slightly; Diarmuid has always had a penchant for the dramatic, and this evening's dress code is no exception. I'm clad in a dress that combines a stark black base with shimmering silver accents—a celestial mimicry of the night sky. Selene has opted for dark blue adorned with gold, as if she's the dusk to my midnight.

The sound of footsteps draws my attention upward, and Diarmuid descends the stairs. His suit is as white as moonlight, tailored in a way that's slightly off from traditional stylings—a nod, perhaps, to whatever mysterious ceremony awaits us tonight. He looks every bit the part of an ethereal host, and my heart skips a beat despite my intentions.

As we step into the limousine ordered by Diarmuid to take us to the mansion, a familiar unease settles over me. Though I've visited the Hands of the King's house before, something about tonight feels different, more ominous. My leg begins to bounce, an involuntary response to the growing anxiety. Selene places a gentle touch on my arm, a silent gesture of solidarity, and Diarmuid's hand comes to rest reassuringly on my knee. His touch is warm, grounding, and for a fleeting moment, I revel in the comfort it brings.

Yet, the irony of the situation isn't lost on me. Here I am, drawing solace from the very man I'm trying to charm, flanked by the woman I must outshine.

The entire situation is difficult for me to process. As the limo pulls up to the grand front door of the manse, I find myself clutching Diarmuid's left arm for support, while Selene, with a grace that matches her carefully chosen attire, takes his right. Diarmuid leads us—a trio representing the dark skies above—toward the entrance.

This isn't the setting of a Regency romance with an orchestra serenading the arrival of the heroine and her love. Although there is indeed an orchestra, and a few heads turn our way as we enter, their gazes are not filled with kindness or admiration. Instead, they are sharp, assessing, filled with the unspoken tension of competition. These are not admirers but rivals, each calculating their own chances in whatever game we are about to play.

Diarmuid ushers us past the doorman and a cluster of gossiping attendees in the front corridor, taking us into the main gathering room. The ceiling here is adorned with tulle, draped so elegantly it almost resembles a soft, cloudy night sky. At some point, Diarmuid's arm leaves mine, but I barely register the loss. My attention is wholly captured by the transformation of the space around us.

The lights twinkle above like distant stars, the soft illumination making the room unrecognizable from the one we had been in during the Dinner of Influence a few weeks prior. The sheer difference is jarring—if I hadn't stood on this very floor before, I would never believe it was the same building. The beauty of it all momentarily distracts me from the uneasy alliances and veiled rivalries that brought us here tonight.

Before I fully grasp what's happening, Selene's hand grips mine, pulling me away with an urgency that nearly makes me stumble in my elaborate gown. Her whispered words are lost in the buzz of the gathering, a murmur of greetings and laughter that she navigates with an ease that leaves me trailing awkwardly behind. I manage only a series of strained smiles, hoping they're convincing enough not to make me stand out in a bad way.

At last, we stop at a seemingly random door along a secluded corridor. It's locked. Selene, with a flick of her wrist, begins to unpin her hair, withdrawing several hairpins before she starts picking the lock. I can't hide my shock.

"What are you doing?!" I hiss, glancing nervously down the corridor.

"Shhhh. People are still arriving. We don't have much time," Selene murmurs, her focus unwavering.

"You are going to get us in trouble!" My voice is a blend of worry and disbelief.

Selene doesn't even look up. "Well, if you're so worried about getting in trouble, you better keep watch. I'm doing this regardless of your help."

The resolution in her tone and the set of her jaw tells me arguing would be pointless. With a frustrated groan, I move to the end of the hallway, positioning myself as a lookout. I pretend to be engrossed in a painting on the wall—a vague landscape that, under any other circumstances, wouldn't hold my attention for more than a second.

"How close are you, Selene?" I call out quietly; my voice tinged with both impatience and a growing curiosity about what she expects to find behind this forbidden door.

"I would be closer if I could concentrate," Selene mutters, her focus interrupted by my question. I can't help feeling like time stretches these moments into eternity, each second lingering longer than it should. I keep my composure as best I can, nodding politely at passersby who glance my way, their eyes curious or indifferent.

Finally, after a soft click and a triumphant whisper from Selene, we slip through the now unlocked door. The room beyond is clearly an office, dominated by an oversized desk that seems too large for the space. Laptops line the shelves, their indicator lights glowing a steady green, charged and ready for use. Books—a sea of hardbacks—fill the rest of the shelves, giving the room an air of stern academia.

As Selene begins to rifle through the desk, papers shuffle, and drawers slam, each sound sharply echoing in the otherwise silent room. I watch her, anxiety mounting with each careless motion.

"What are you looking for?" I ask, unable to mask the concern in my voice.

"I don't know. Something. Anything," she replies, her voice a mix of frustration and desperation.

Her hands move quickly, too quickly. Papers are turned over, drawers are pulled out too far. Everything about her search is messy, chaotic. My heart races; the disorder of it all feels dangerous. This isn't the calculated risk of a seasoned schemer; this is the panic-driven search of someone grasping for a lifeline. The anxiety that had been simmering within me begins to boil over. The urge to flee, to escape the potential disaster we are spiraling toward almost consumes me.

But I stand frozen, watching Selene, knowing that despite my fears, leaving now could mean missing a crucial discovery—or worse, facing whatever consequences may come alone.

If Selene messes this up, it won't just be her who pays the price. I can feel the heavy responsibility weighing on me, the grim possibility that Ella might suffer for our recklessness. I plead with Selene, my voice barely a whisper, "We need to leave, now."

But she's motionless, fixated on something small and gleaming in her hand—a discovery that has captivated her completely. In a flash of sudden movement, a bookshelf to our side creaks open like a secret passage, but Selene, quick as a shadow, slips the mysterious item into the top of her dress for safekeeping.

Realizing the imminent danger, I rush over, slamming the swinging bookshelf shut with my body. There's a startled pause from the other side, then a forceful push against it. The bookshelf trembles under the impact, books tumbling down in a chaotic cascade.

"Get it closed!" I hiss to Selene, who shoves the heavy desk toward the bookshelves. Every inch she moves seems to take an eternity, and the urgency is suffocating.

"Shhhh. Don't let them hear your voice," she hisses back, her eyes wide with a mix of fear and determination.

"Hurry. Please," I urge Selene, desperation creeping into my voice as the pressure against the bookshelf intensifies.

"This is harder than it looks," Selene grunts, her face flushed with exertion as she heaves the desk inch by agonizing inch toward the bookshelf. Seeing an opportunity, I let go of the bookshelf and rush to her side, throwing my weight against the heavy furniture. It slides into place just in time, a makeshift barricade that barely holds as the unseen assailant on the other side continues to push, their frustration evident in the force of their efforts. The bookshelf creaks ominously, but it holds.

Without another word, we flee the room, our breaths ragged and hearts racing.

"What a rush!" Selene exclaims with a laugh as we merge

with the flow of guests in the main room, her exhilaration a stark contrast against my pounding fear.

I grab Selene by the shoulder, spinning her around to face me. Her laughter fades as she sees the serious expression on my face.

"I don't know what you were thinking, but that was reckless," I scold her, my voice low but intense.

Selene's smile falters, replaced by a nonchalant shrug. "Relax. If they find out it was me, I'll take the fall."

Her cavalier attitude stokes my frustration. "It won't just be you," I snap back. "You may want to throw your life away, but some of us have something to fight for. Don't get me involved in your schemes without letting me be a part of the planning process."

"I'm sorry. You're right. I should have considered your situation," Selene concedes, her tone genuine, but it does little to quell the storm of emotions swirling within me.

As I scan the room, I notice staff members whispering and darting their eyes around, a clear sign they know something's amiss. A knot of fear tightens in my stomach. Every carefully calculated move I've made to protect my sister could unravel because of Selene's impulsive foray behind a locked door. The fact that Selene came prepared with hairpins and lock-picking skills gnaws at me—this wasn't just a spur-of-the-moment decision.

The room's lights dim, pulling my thoughts back to the present. Diarmuid makes his way through the crowd, leaving his brothers behind. He takes Selene's arm and mine, drawing us close as we join the gathering at the front of the room. His presence, solid and reassuring, makes me feel slightly safer. If our misadventure comes to light, I find a shred of hope in believing Diarmuid might protect us.

A deep, resonant gong sounds once, then again, and once more, echoing through the grand room. Hooded figures begin to assemble, creating a sense of foreboding. Lorcan, Diarmuid's oldest brother, strides toward the stage with an air of authority. Then, as if on cue, the wall shifts and opens.

Out steps Victor, The Hand himself.

My breath catches in my throat at the sight of him. Victor's arrival means that whatever is happening here is more significant and perhaps more dangerous than any of us anticipated. As he takes the stage, the atmosphere thickens with anticipation and unease. I grip Diarmuid's arm a little tighter, trying to steady myself against the surge of fear and the weight of what might come next. This night, it seems, is far from over, and the stakes are higher than ever.

89

CHAPTER TEN

The lights dim around me, fading to a near whisper of illumination. A celestial theme reigns tonight; every surface is either shimmering with sequins or sparkling with glitter, casting a soft glow that makes the room look like a starlit sky. I can barely make out the faces around me—some familiar, some strangers—yet each carries the weight of importance tonight.

Lorcan steps onto the stage, and the subtle shift in the room's energy draws every eye to him. He embodies the essence of a politician, with a solemn grace that belies his years, though a ghost of a smile plays at the corners of his mouth. It's clear he wasn't born for this role, but he has been shaped and molded by the demands and expectations of the order. He's a silent storm, commanding attention without a word, something I've always struggled with.

As I linger in the shadows, I watch him, aware of the vast gulf that lies between his presence and mine. I've never been one to attract attention—couldn't afford it, in fact. It's safer to observe rather than being observed.

"Ladies and gentlemen," Lorcan begins, his voice reverberating softly through the hushed room, "welcome to the evening of the Harvest Moon." He pauses, allowing the significance of the event to settle among us. "Though the moon appeared later than usual this year, its significance remains unchanged. Tonight, we celebrate the fruits of our labors, the culmination of another year's hard work and dedication."

I shift slightly, the mention of labor and dedication resonating uncomfortably within me. My contributions are less tangible, harder to celebrate.

Lorcan continues. "We also honor the memory of the first emperor in human history, Sargon of Akkad, who reigned from 2334 to 2279 BC in the city of Ur." Murmurs of respect ripple through the crowd, a collective acknowledgment of our roots in power and leadership. "As the inaugural emperor, Sargon set the standards by which all great leaders are measured. His legacy is not merely historical but foundational to the ethos of our order."

I find myself unexpectedly caught up in the narrative, imagining the vast stretches of time that connect us back to Sargon. Lorcan's next words draw a direct line from the past to the present. "Significantly, Sargon's daughter served as a priestess to the Ur moon god, Sin, anchoring our ceremony tonight in ancient tradition. Sin, the shepherd of the heavens, guides us as we, the leaders and shepherds of humanity, endeavor to guide our flock toward a prosperous future."

Solemnity falls upon the room, a shared sense of purpose wrapping around us like a cloak.

Lorcan's voice continues to fill the room, a soothing drone that contrasts sharply with the storm brewing inside me. My eyes are fixed on Victor, standing off to the side of the stage. There's an ease about him that irks me, a confidence wrapped securely in layers of loyalty and protection. His guards, a constant shadow, form a barrier I've never dared breach. Not yet. My own life still holds some value to me. But I imagine a day when that might change, and Victor would be left defenseless against whatever storm I might bring.

Lost in these dark thoughts, I startle when a gentle touch grazes my arm. It's Selene. She always seems to know when my emotions are teetering on the edge. Her presence is comforting, unlike Niamh's, which often feels distant and disconnected. Selene's touch brings me back from the brink, grounding me, though the anger continues to simmer just beneath my skin.

As Lorcan extols the virtues of our ancient predecessors, Selene's grip tightens momentarily—a silent communication of concern. My gaze is still locked on Victor when the murmur of late arrivals pulls the attention of the room. I try to ignore them, to focus on the danger I know, but Selene's insistent tug on my sleeve is impossible to ignore.

Reluctantly, I turn, and my gaze clashes with Wolf's. He's unmistakable, arrogance is etched into every line of his face. Amira on his arm adds to the image of smug self-satisfaction. The sight of him ignites something reckless within me, a fiery surge that drowns out Selene's whispered warnings.

Before I fully register my actions, I'm moving across the room, propelled by a mix of rage and a thirst for confrontation. The room falls into hushed anticipation as I approach.

With no words exchanged, I close the gap, and without hesitation, my fist connects with Wolf's face. The impact sends a shock through my arm, but it's nothing compared to the shockwave that ripples through the room. Wolf stumbles back, surprise morphing into fury as he touches a hand to his bleeding nose.

He's quiet for a moment; then he pushes Amira aside, someone catching her before she falls, and he swings at me.

I grin as I dance back and land another solid hit to his face.

"Stop!" Lorcan's voice roars across the room. But I am beyond stopping. I want blood. I swing again, only to be pulled back by guards, others arriving to grab Wolf and halt his advance toward me.

Victor's voice slices through the tense silence like a blade. Everyone in the grand room freezes, the chaos momentarily suspended as his cold, authoritative tone commands the space. "What an honor for us to witness such a struggle on this night, the night where we honor the legacy of Sargon of Akkad. A Duke has challenged a King just as Sargon challenged the kingdom of Ellam."

His eyes, icy and calculating, survey the room, stopping to linger on the men holding Wolf and me apart. With a subtle nod, the men reluctantly step back, though their bodies remain tensed, ready to intervene at the slightest hint of renewed aggression.

Victor continues, his gaze now locked on me, making the air around me feel colder, heavier. "In the spirit of our illustrious forebears, let this conflict unfold as it must. Let it be decided not by whispers in dark corners, but by the will and strength of those involved. This is how leaders are tested. This is how their worth is proven."

Wolf and I eye each other warily. The brief respite allows the adrenaline to settle, replaced by a cold realization of the spectacle we've become. Victor's words hang between us, a challenge and a decree. The room remains deathly silent; every member of the order present now is a witness to this unexpected trial by combat.

Lorcan's earlier attempts to restore order are forgotten, his authority overshadowed by Victor's commanding presence. I can see frustration mixed with concern etch his features, knowing full well the implications of letting this conflict play out in such a public and symbolic manner.

As the room watches, I weigh my options. Fighting Wolf might prove my strength, but at what cost? And backing down could show weakness, potentially as dangerous. Selene's earlier touch on my arm echoes in my memory, a reminder of the stakes not just for me but for those connected to me.

Voices erupt around us as everyone waits and watches to see what will happen next.

Victor's voice, sharp and unyielding, slices through the murmurs of the crowd again. "Please, gentlemen, continue your battle." His command is an echo of darker times, a familiar coldness that sends a shiver down my spine, reigniting memories of harsh lessons etched into my skin.

Everyone takes a step back. As the space between Wolf and me widens, we both shed our dinner jackets, the heavy fabric hitting the floor with a soft thud. The room seems to hold its breath, the atmosphere charged with a palpable tension.

Wolf and I face each other, not just as two men, but as legacies of a ruthless upbringing. Raised in the mafia, forged in violence and survival, we learned the language of power through fists and blood from an early age. We both understand the unspoken rules of such confrontations—there are no winners, only survivors.

As I look up, trying to glean some hint of what might be going through Victor's mind, his face gives nothing away. It's a mask of stoicism, carved from stone, his eyes reflecting nothing but the dim light of the shimmering room. Around us, whispers flutter like uneasy birds, their words indistinct but their curiosity clear.

Victor's plans for us remain shrouded in mystery, but it's evident he's orchestrated this moment, counting on it to unfold according to his unseen design. Whatever outcome he desires, I know it hinges on what happens next between Wolf and me.

The memories of past beatings are vivid in my mind as I face Wolf, the sharp sting of blood and the clammy stickiness of fabric against my wounds serving as brutal reminders of what it means to lose. A voice in my head, an echo of a past mentor or perhaps my own survival instinct, whispers fiercely, *"Kings must not bend, Diarmuid. You must not be defeated."*

Clenching my fists tighter, I brace myself. This isn't just a fight; it's a testament to my place in this order, a declaration of my strength and my refusal to bow down. I meet Wolf's gaze, seeing in his eyes the same determination, the same unwillingness to yield.

The silence stretches taut as a bowstring before I finally move, stepping forward to meet him in the center.

Wolf charges, his form blurring the line between human and beast, his heavy breaths a guttural soundtrack to his primal aggression. I steel myself, lowering my stance, spreading my feet for stability. I'm ready—or as ready as one can be.

Wolf's momentum is like a freight train, but I've been here before, countless times. The impact is immense, a collision of force and intent, but I use his momentum against him, twisting my body at the last second. My training kicks in, muscle memory guiding me as I redirect him, sending him staggering past me. The crowd gasps, a ripple of surprise at the deft maneuver.

But Wolf is relentless. He recovers and comes at me again, fury written in every line of his body. His fists fly. I raise my arms, blocking, deflecting, absorbing the blows. Each strike sends a shock wave of pain through my arms, but I grit my teeth against it. His persistence is animalistic, but it lacks precision.

Don't just stand there! Move! The internal command snaps me back to focus. I can't win by defense alone.

I shift my weight, stepping to the side as Wolf throws another heavy punch, his momentum carrying him forward as I move.

It's an opening—brief but clear. I counter with a swift jab to his ribs, the connection solid. Wolf grunts, the sound pained, and for a moment, his assault pauses.

Seizing the moment, I unleash a series of targeted strikes, aiming for vulnerabilities—ribs, stomach, kidneys. With each hit, I can feel the tide turning, his breaths becoming more labored, his movements slower.

Focus, Diarmuid. Control. The mental admonition steadies me. This isn't just a brawl; it's a test of everything I've learned, everything I've endured. It's about proving my place here, under Victor's cold scrutiny, and demonstrating that I'm more than just another soldier in his ranks.

Wolf staggers back, winded and weakened, and I prepare for another advance. He charges, and I twist again, sticking out my leg to knock him down. Wolf does his own twist and catches my foot in his hand. He lifts my foot with a strength he shouldn't possess and sends me sailing to the floor.

Get up, you piece of shit!

The inner voice has me rising again, and Wolf strikes. I block and jab at his ribs—one, two, three times. Wolf staggers back, and I dance from foot to foot, waiting for him to attack again.

He wipes blood from his face and makes a dive to the left, away from me. I pause, thinking he may be running, but instead, he grabs a knife from one of the nearby tables. The glint on its tip is cast from the overhead lighting. He's racing toward me, slashing the air, practically foaming at the mouth in his frenzy and need to win.

I retreat but never turn my back to him; there are no weapons near me. I drop to the ground and retrieve my suit jacket. The moment I rise, Wolf strikes with the knife.

With one quick movement, I wrap the jacket around the knife. I twist with all my strength, and the knife is released, like a small present inside my jacket that I retrieve.

I don't slow down but grip Wolf's arm. Twisting him, I bring his back to my chest and the blade to his throat.

"STOP!" Victor's voice booms across the room.

I'm panting, adrenaline racing through my veins, and the need to open Wolf's throat in front of everyone has me wanting to finish the job.

But I must obey Victor's command.

I want to disobey him so badly. Maybe he sees it in my eyes because he shakes his head.

"Diarmuid has won and retained his position as King," Victor announces with an authoritative tone that brooks no argument. "However, Wolf is no longer a Duke. He is demoted to Marquess. Amira shall return to Diarmuid."

The weight of Victor's words hangs heavily in the room, a tangible shift in the power dynamics that leaves no room for doubt about the consequences of tonight's events. I release Wolf, and he falls to the floor.

Amira rushes to Wolf's side, her movements betraying a mix of relief and despair. Her face, when she turns to look at me, is a canvas of conflict—her desire to come to me, battling with her urge to escape the life bound by these brutal contests of power.

Her eyes, wide and searching, flicker to Selene and Niamh, who now stand beside me. It's clear the thought of joining this fray holds little appeal to her, the realization dawning that her return might not bring the solace she seeks. She helps Wolf rise, and he accepts her arm.

As I watch her struggle, a decision forms in my mind, clear and sharp amid the chaos. She doesn't want me, she wants him.

"Amira is officially released from her obligations to me," I declare, my voice firm, carrying across the silent room. "She is free to return with Wolf."

It's a release for her.

I turn to Wolf, who is still regaining his composure, his eyes dark with humiliation and brewing anger. "Leave," I say, my tone leaving no room for argument.

The room's atmosphere shifts again. The members of the order watch as Wolf, now stripped of his former prestige, gathers his pride and exits with Amira. Their departure is quiet, marked by the shame of defeat and the heavy steps of the demoted. Amira takes one final look at me. I'm not sure if it's hate, hurt, or relief in her eyes.

As the doors close behind them, the weight of the evening's events settles on my shoulders. I know this isn't the end. Wolf's demotion and public humiliation will fester, a wound that will no doubt drive him toward thoughts of vengeance. I must be ready. The game of power we play is never over; it merely pauses, gathering tension like a coiled spring.

Turning back to the room, I meet the gazes of Selene and

Niamh. Their expressions are a mix of relief and concern. I am aware of the repercussions that tonight will bring. We need to prepare, to strengthen our defenses and alliances. Tonight, I have maintained my position, but the battle lines have been redrawn, and the next confrontation is only a matter of time.

Victor watches all this with an inscrutable gaze, perhaps pleased with the way the play for power unfolded under his control. As the room slowly begins to murmur again, the sound of conversation rising like a tentative wave, I know that despite the victory, the true challenges are just beginning.

CHAPTER ELEVEN

Selene

The morning light seeps through the blinds, casting long shadows across the floor. I can still feel the emptiness on Diarmuid's side of the bed, the coolness of the sheets where he should be. Last night, after we returned from the gala, I had reached out to him, searching for a connection, something to assure me that we were still us. But his kisses felt mechanical, as if he was there in body alone, his mind miles away.

I lay there, nestled under the blankets, watching his silhouette against the moonlit window. He stayed just long enough to convince himself I was asleep, then slipped away. Where he went, I couldn't say. It wasn't the first time, but the sting of his absence never dulled.

The routine of the morning unfolds automatically. Niamh, ever the disciplined one, cuts through the water in the heated pool outside, her strokes steady and strong. I sit at the kitchen table, the newspaper spread out before me, the crossword half-completed. My pencil taps against the paper. I miss my grandparents. I've continued this tradition here in Diarmuid's home, but it doesn't feel the same without the puzzle filled in from my grandfather's earlier attempt to complete it before I arrived.

The black and white squares fail to distract me from my swirling thoughts of last night. Why did Amira leave with Wolf? Was she happy with him? She didn't look happy, yet she never did. Niamh's approaching footsteps have me looking up from the puzzle. The familiar sound of her entering the kitchen, the fridge opening, the rustle of her preparing her usual post-swim protein shake—it's comforting, yet today, it feels different.

"Niamh, come join me," I call out, keeping my voice light, casual. It's a tone I've mastered over the years, hiding the tremble that threatens to betray my calm exterior.

She rounds the corner, a towel draped around her neck, her hair slicked back from the water. "What's up?" she asks, a note of cheer in her voice that grates on my current mood.

I pat the spot next to me on the couch, and she pads over in her bare feet, settling down with her shake in hand. "Nothing much, just thought we could catch up a bit. You know, like old times."

She nods, sipping her shake, her eyes scanning my face. "Everything okay?"

I hesitate, the words catching in my throat. "It's Diarmuid,"

I finally admit. The name feels heavy on my tongue. "He's been so distant lately. Last night... I don't know, it felt like he was a million miles away."

Niamh sets her shake down, her expression softening. "I noticed he left early this morning. Didn't say where he was going."

The cushions give a soft sigh as Niamh settles next to me, the familiar whiff of chlorine lingering around her like a faint halo. It's a reminder of her new dedication, a twice-a-day ritual in the pool since Diarmuid bought the house for us. Her transformation is evident, the swimmer's build replacing the delicate lines of her former dancer's physique. It's a change I've watched with a mixture of pride and relief. Niamh finally has the space to pursue what she loves, free from her mother's relentless push toward ballet.

She takes a sip from her sports bottle, the thick protein shake likely vanilla-flavored—her favorite. My eyes flick to the notebook on my lap, my fingers subtly pulling a small object from my pocket. It's a bronze medallion. I set it on the notebook carefully, making sure it's shielded from any prying eyes. Despite Diarmuid's assurances of privacy, I've never quite shaken off the paranoia that there might be cameras hidden even here, in the cozy corners of our living room.

Niamh's touch is gentle on the bronze medallion, her fingers tracing the inscribed words. "luíonn an dorn ag Sí an Bhrú." Above this cryptic message, the Hands of Kings is stamped prominently—a forward palm with a crown resting in its center, a symbol that has grown more significant and enigmatic since it first appeared in our lives. Despite its weight, the medallion feels like a key to something ancient and hidden.

We've developed a routine for moments like this when the walls might have ears and the shadows might watch. Silence becomes our fortress as we reach for our phones, opening the notepad apps to converse in a way that leaves no room for eavesdroppers.

I type swiftly, the screen's glow casting light on our hushed faces.

It keeps showing up. There has to be a connection we're missing.

Niamh nods, her brows furrowed as she taps out her response, the click of her fingers on the screen punctuating the silence.

It's those symbols again.

I nod, meeting Niamh's gaze before I refocus on the phone in my hand. **I don't have the other symbols here, but they look *exactly* like the symbols I found before.**

Niamh is quick to respond. **Do you have a plan to get to your apartment?**

I shake my head. I'm not light on my feet like Niamh, so getting to my apartment unnoticed isn't something I'm sure I can master alone. But I'm not alone.

I'll help you get away, Niamh texts, her words a lifeline thrown across the digital divide.

Her idea of "help" is formed from her own escape a few days earlier. She had locked her room, opened her window, and shimmied down to the lawn. Once she was outside, she scaled the wall to freedom. I'm not out of shape, but I'm certainly no Niamh.

Standing on my balcony, I grip the railing, my palms slick with sweat. "This is it. I'm going to die here." My heart races as I begin my descent. Every muscle in my body protests with fear and adrenaline mingling in a potent cocktail.

By some stroke of divine luck, my feet find the softness of the grass below. The relief is short-lived as I grapple with the wall, my grunts loud in the silent night. When I control my breathing, I glance back up at my bedroom window; Niamh hangs over the sill with two thumbs raised and a smile on her face. I smile back before I cross the lawn, sticking to the shadows. I can't help but allow some dark thoughts to enter my mind, like, what if Niamh helped me to get rid of me? I scold myself for thinking of her like that when she has been a rock through all of this.

Yet, the knowledge that this is a competition doesn't alleviate the dark thought completely.

Scaling the second wall leaves me exhausted, and when I finally take my seat on the bus, I expect the ride to lull me into sleep. But the hum of the engine and the rocking motion do little to quiet the whirlwind of thoughts in my head.

Darkness has cast a blanket across my grandparents' home. The bus passes it and stops only a few meters away.

Clutching the medallion tightly in my hand, I skip past my grandparents' house entirely. My feet carry me up the stairs to the apartment above their garage. I fumble with the keys, my fingers clumsy and trembling. The door swings open with a soft creak, and I flick on the light.

To my utter shock, Diarmuid and Niamh are sitting right there, waiting for me.

I'm stunned, my mind racing through calculations, trying to puzzle out how they could have possibly gotten here before me. As if reading my thoughts, Diarmuid answers, his voice calm and steady.

"I had just come home when you made it to the lawn. I watched from the balcony while you climbed the wall."

"You watched me?" My voice is a mixture of disbelief and irritation.

Diarmuid smiles, a hint of solemnity in his gaze. "I'm always watching you, pet. It's my duty. I am your King."

His words hang in the air, heavy and full of unspoken promises and secrets, as I try to wrap my head around this new reality.

That explains why Diarmuid beat me here; I was constrained to the pace of public transport while he sped away in his car. But still, the nagging question remains—how did he know where I was going?

I glance at Niamh, seeking an ally or perhaps an answer, but she avoids my gaze, her eyes fixed on some distant point.

"Don't redirect on her. Look at me. Talk to me," Diarmuid commands, his voice firm, brooking no evasion. "Now, what was my rule about leaving the estate?"

"Not without your express permission," I reply, the words bitter as they leave my lips.

"Yet?" His single word hangs between us like a challenge.

"I left without your permission," I admit, my voice steady despite the churn of emotions inside me.

"Why?"

"Because this is important to me." I meet his gaze, defiance kindling within me.

Diarmuid stands and begins to pace the apartment, his movements deliberate. He pauses occasionally to examine the photos, notes, and information connected by red string that adorn the walls—my private thoughts laid bare.

"What is your goal here, Selene?" he asks, turning to face me once again, his expression unreadable.

Did I have a real goal? Everything felt so overwhelming. The revelations about the real power structure of the cult, understanding the extent of the O'Sullivan mafia family's influence, and unraveling the mystery of what happened to Sofia Hughes—all of it pulled me in multiple directions. On top of that, Diarmuid's nonexistent explanation about why murdering his uncle was absolutely necessary and the cryptic words Isaac Waryn whispered to me at the Diners of Influence Dinner only added to my confusion.

Diarmuid had been given the grim task of murdering a child. Just the thought sent a shiver down my spine.

After discovering that my entire existence had been orchestrated—that I was created and raised solely to serve as payment to the order—I felt a desperate need to cling to anything that might offer a semblance of purpose or identity. Yet, here, in the presence of Diarmuid, these personal revelations felt too dangerous, too vulnerable to share.

So, I couldn't tell Diarmuid any of this—none of it.

Silence hangs heavy as I wrestle with my thoughts, unsure of how to articulate the storm inside without revealing too much.

Diarmuid turns and looks at me, his gaze sharp and analytical. He's a master at reading people; I've witnessed it countless times when associates visited our house. He would sit back, let them speak, and then, with uncanny precision, he'd turn the conversation on its head. He could read people better than most could read a restaurant menu.

I try to keep my face blank, my eyes void of the storm brewing within. He tilts his head slightly and smiles—a smile that hints at amusement or, perhaps, a touch of condescension.

Finally, he says, "You don't know why you are doing this."

The statement hangs in the air, echoing against the walls, filling the room with its inescapable truth.

Diarmuid turns back to my research scattered across the room. His voice is calm yet carries an edge of warning, "This is dangerous, pet. It's an unsecured location. The information you have here… there are people who will kill you for knowing this."

His words strike a chord of fear, yet they also reinforce the gravity of what I've stumbled upon. Every document, every note I've connected with red string, holds a piece of a larger puzzle.

I'm well aware of the dangers, but that hasn't been enough to deter me. The urgency of uncovering the truth, of peeling back the layers of deceit and manipulation, outweighs my fear.

"All of this needs to be packed up," Diarmuid declares with finality. "The three of us will set this up in the study at our home. I will install a digital lock on the door. And you will accept my assistance in this."

His words come as a surprise. I know the information I'm digging into could be severely damaging to the order. Diarmuid, as much as he benefits from being a King within this intricate hierarchy, should be the last person wanting to aid me. Why would he help, unless there's something more, some reason he, too, finds it worth risking everything to unearth the truth?

Weeks ago, before the estate was purchased, we had made promises to support each other, to be on the same team. Now, standing here, watching him take decisive steps to safeguard both me and my research, is the first real indication that those weren't just empty promises.

This is the first time I actually feel that the three of us—Diarmuid, Niamh, and I—are truly on the same page. This shared commitment, at last, visible and tangible, stirs a mix of relief and renewed determination in me.

I'm not sure if it's relief or just a want for Diarmuid that has me reaching up on the tip of my toes and pressing my lips against his. "Thank you." The kiss is gentle, and I know it comes from a deeper place than just lust for this man; I think I'm falling for him, which is dangerous in so many ways. Yet when he deepens the kiss, I sink into him. Our bodies hard against each other, close enough that I can feel his excitement pressed against my stomach. My core tightens with a need, and I'm pulling at his suit jacket; he yanks his tie off without breaking the kiss, but when he does, his eyes are feverish. Maybe it's what I want to see there, or maybe it's really there, but in his gaze, I see something also deeper than lust, something protective, something primal, and I want him to consume me. His hands reach out and grip the base of my top, pulling it swiftly over my head. My breasts swell in my bra, and when his large hands run along the side, I close my eyes and let his touch consume me; each stroke feels like fire, and when his kisses trail down my neck, I inhale deeply; his scent is all around me. Another set of hands rests on my hips and it's then that I remember Niamh is in the room. I almost forgot. Guilt has me stepping aside, allowing her to see Diarmuid. His gaze seems to flicker to Niamh as if he also forgot she was here. Once again, I think that may be wishful thinking.

I want to hit stop on my thoughts and just enjoy Diarmuid's touch. His hands snake to the back of Niamh's neck, dragging her closer, and I find myself watching him kissing her, wondering if the kiss feels the same to him and her.

I'm getting in my head again, and to stop the thoughts, I take off my boots and jeans. My movements pull Diarmuid away from Niamh, and with fluid movements, he unbuttons his shirt. I love that he trusts us, allowing us to see his damaged back, not hiding his flaws from us. To me, they are a testament to his strength and a reminder that he can endure anything.

My double bed in the apartment isn't as big or as luxurious as what we are used to in Diarmuid's home, but it will serve its purpose here tonight.

I step forward as Niamh starts to remove her clothes, and I grip Diarmuid's belt. Yanking it open. He doesn't help but watch me as he drags a hand through his hair. Pulling his trousers and boxers down to his ankles, he kicks off his shoes and removes everything. He's glorious and so much a man standing in front of me.

His erection always takes me by surprise, and I clench my thighs together remembering what it feels like to have him fill me completely.

I glance at Niamh, who's naked, and I remove my bra and panties. Nothing is covering us now. And as one, myself and Niamh step toward Diarmuid. Niamh starts kissing him, and he immediately touches her breast. I find my way to my knees, taking the tip of his cock in my mouth, running my tongue along the swollen head. It jerks in my mouth, and I hold his cock firm with my hand as I work my mouth up and down his shaft; he jerks his body forward, trying to go deeper, but I can never take all of him without gagging. I try, but his cock is too big.

I reach around and let my free hand touch his hard balls. I squeeze and pull them enough for him to moan into his mouth but not too hard to cause him pain.

When his hand touches the crown of my head, I know he wants me up, and I let his cock out of my mouth that's coated in my saliva and stand.

"Both of you lie on the bed." He gives his shaft a few hard strokes, and we obediently lie on the bed. There isn't room for Diarmuid to join us.

"Spread your legs," he says, still stroking his cock.

I'm wet, and I do as he commands.

Our legs dangling over the edge, the brush of Niamh's thigh against mine as I look at her. She's as excited as I am. I don't think I could ever get enough of Diarmuid.

When he kneels, he places a hand on both our thighs. He starts with Niamh, his head going between her legs, and he starts to lick; her eyes slam closed, and she bites her lip.

Diarmuid's hand trails up my leg and stops when it rests on my hump; his thumb expertly starts touching my clit. My body is on fire, my mind a frenzy of need. I grip my nipple and squeeze while jerking my hips up, forcing his hand lower. He slips two fingers inside me, but it's brief. He shifts quickly, and his mouth sucks my clit; it's my turn to cry out as his tongue waggles quickly over my opening. I know it's Niamh's hand that touches my breast, and I keep my eyes closed, enjoying all the sensations that grow heavier inside me.

Niamh's touch, which I'm almost becoming accustomed to, squeezes my nipple, rolling it between her thumb and forefinger.

I cry out again as Diarmuid's tongue goes deeper inside me. I want more. I want him inside me. When he removes his mouth, my eyes flicker open, and he's standing stroking his cock, watching Niamh fondle my breasts. Niamh has grown so much bolder, and she leans over me, pressing a kiss to my mouth. Her kisses are soft, and when her tongue darts into my mouth, I slip my tongue into hers.

Large hands grip my thighs, and I'm yanked lower on the bed as Diarmuid raises my hips and moves in between my thighs.

The tip of his cock rests at my opening, and I sink my tongue deeper into Niamh's' mouth. I reach out and touch her breast; her nipples are hard, and I run a single finger across it, scrapping it with a nail; she moans into my mouth as Diarmuid thrusts inside me. His movements are frantic, and he stretches the walls as far as they can go. There is always a sense of pain when he fills me, but it's overridden by my excitement. Niamh breaks the kiss, and I release her breasts as she rises to her knees and crawls over to Diarmuid. With one hand in his hair, she kisses him, but he keeps his eyes open, watching me as he pounds inside me.

I hold his gaze, pulling my legs up with my hands, giving him more access. Each pound sends shockwaves through my system. Watching Niamh kiss him, turns me on so much, but knowing he is watching me gives me a rush that I've never felt before.

He breaks the kiss with Niamh to focus on me.

"Touch yourself." He commands Niamh. She lies back down beside me, and her hand slips between her legs as she starts to circle her clit.

"Come for me, pet," Diarmuid says.

I'm not sure if the command is for me or Niamh, but it's enough for me to raise my legs as high as I possibly can. Any reservations he had, he releases, and he fucks me like a drowning man, moving so quickly, keeping both of us afloat.

Niamh's pants grow louder, and I know she's close to coming, so am I.

"Fuck!" Diarmuid's word and his quick thrusts let me know

he's close to my excitement nearly bubbles over, but I want to see his face as he comes inside me.

Niamh cries out as she comes on her finger.

"Good girl," Diarmuid says to Niamh.

He moves quicker inside me. The sound of our heavy breathing and flesh slapping against flesh has me digging my nails into my thighs that I hold up. He cries out as he fills me with his cream, but he doesn't slow, allowing me to come with him. We ride high, and I close my eyes as a burst of light flashes behind my lids.

My body shudders with each explosion, and when Diarmuid slows down and pulls out of me, I'm still fighting to stabilize my breath.

I lower my legs down, and when I open my eyes, Diarmuid is looking at me, and I swear I see something loving in them.

My cheeks heat, and I glance away. Too many emotions are spinning.

"We better pack everything up." Niamh declares as she slips off the bed, and I think I detect a note of disappointment.

As Niamh gets dressed, Diarmuid reaches out his hand to help me rise. When I'm standing beside him, I'm surprised with the light brush of his lips against mine. It's words not spoken and words I'm not ready to hear.

We get tidied up and dressed, and then, without any words, we start packing up all the research.

After what feels like a few hours, I hand Diarmuid the last bit of research, and he reaches past me to flick off the light to the empty-looking apartment.

CHAPTER TWELVE

Amira

As I sit at my new desk, the stack of photographs before me feels heavier than mere paper should. Wolf's generosity—or perhaps strategy—has granted me an office space adjacent to his own. The quiet here is thick, a contrast to the chaos that has engulfed our lives since the Harvest Moon Ball. Since that night, Wolf has been different: incapacitated yet unpredictably violent and alarmingly insatiable. I wince, remembering how my hair became his favored leash as he took what he wanted from me in the bedroom. He was never gentle; I was starting to believe he was incapable of anything but volatile and violent movements. Most times, he took me from behind, never wanting to look at me.

Or maybe he didn't want me to see him. To see the monster that lurked under his flesh. But I saw it; I didn't need to see his eyes to know he was rotten to the core. His darkness was so deep that I swear there wasn't much human left in him anymore. In my times of need, I would try to reach out to that more humane side of him, but I've never found it, and I don't think I ever will. It's well and truly gone.

Rubbing my neck, I distract myself with the task at hand. Not the million images of him fucking me with a vengeance that hurt so much. I often went to other places in my mind, but his constant hammering into me would pull me back and keep me present.

The photographs spread across my desk show faces too young to be marred by our dark world. Boys and girls, aged ten to fifteen, stare back at me from both poised social media poses and secretive candid shots taken by a long lens. Each image is a stolen moment, a snapshot of a life that might soon be uprooted. Be destroyed by the darkness that has soaked this world, and I fear there is no escape for any of us.

I've never asked Wolf about his ''cargo''—a term that chills me to my core. I've justified my ignorance by imagining these children as unfortunate souls swept away by the poor choices of their parents. But the truth is simpler and far more sinister. These photographs are not just images; they're selections. Choices I am complicit in, as I push some photos aside and draw others closer. Those I choose will soon transition from being vibrant kids to just names and faces on missing posters.

The silence is broken by the subtle click of my office door.

"Miss Amira," the voice belongs to the maid from the hallway, the one who ignored my suffering the first time that Wolf raped me. She has become a target for me, one I enjoy torturing. One I can focus on to take my mind off my own suffering. My small way of gaining back some control.

I press my hand against my leg, feeling the cool metal of the pistol concealed beneath my dress. Wolf's rules are always strict and demeaning; one insists I be presentable and sexy at all times. It's degrading, a rule crafted solely to belittle me. Yet, ironically, it offers the unexpected benefit of making it easier to hide my gun. One I wish I could use on not just Wolf but this maid also. I will have my time.

The maid's gaze meets mine, sharp and judgmental even after the slap I delivered earlier. Clearly, she hasn't learned much, her eyes now scrutinizing me even more critically.

"What is it?" I snap, unable to keep the irritation from bleeding into my tone.

"It's your mother, ma'am," she replies, her voice steady.

Despite my repeated requests to be addressed less formally, she insists on "ma'am" over "miss." It grates on me, adding to the tension already simmering.

"What about my mother?" I ask, my voice tight, bracing for what might come next. The simple mention of my mother always sets my nerves on edge, a cascade of old wounds threatening to reopen.

"She is disturbing the students," the maid explains, her voice low but distinct.

Wolf's downward spiral wasn't just his own demise; it dragged everyone connected to him into the abyss, including my mother and me. His latest experiments with hallucinogens had escalated, pushing my mother beyond her limits until I couldn't bear to watch any longer. Now, her disturbances were becoming a public spectacle. Her screams reaching from the belly of the basement all the way to the first floor where the students were being taught.

Her voice, growing louder even from a distance, pulls at my already strained patience. I narrow my eyes at the maid, my gaze sharp and searching, before setting down the photographs I had been pretending to sort through. They're just another facade in this house of secrets.

"Come with me. I may need your help," I command more than request, standing abruptly.

As we leave the office area and head toward the room where my mother is kept, I notice the staff deliberately avoid eye contact. They whisper to each other, casting furtive glances in our direction as they scurry away. I know the reason behind their unease—it isn't just because of Wolf's infamous treatment of me. It's also because of the woman trailing silently behind me, a part of this twisted scenario yet somehow separate, her presence unsettling even to those accustomed to Wolf's ways.

As I walk with the maid toward my mother's room, the weight of isolation presses down on me. The staff's eyes dart away as they pass, their silent judgment echoing the maid's betrayal. She has turned them against me, a cruel revenge for a moment of anger I had let slip through my control. Now, no matter how violently

Wolf treats me, there is no sympathy to be found among the staff. No one brings washcloths to dab away the tears and blood; no one whispers warnings when he approaches with fury in his eyes. They all turn their backs, leaving me alone to face the storm. But, I brace the storm each time; I'm stronger than any of these foolish women think.

I've done nothing to deserve this abandonment, this collective cold shoulder. Yet, here I am, ostracized within my own home.

When Wolf sobers up, his wrath will undoubtedly be fearsome. He'll be furious that the staff has neglected their duties to care for his prized possession—me. In his twisted world, he is both my tormentor and protector, providing me with the strangest mix of pain and security. It's a bizarre, unsettling balance that keeps me tethered to him.

I know my situation is dire, but I cling to a small comfort: I am the only woman here. Diarmuid had once offered a different life, one that might have been kinder but one where there was no guarantee of permanence. Leaving Wolf meant risking an even more potentially grim fate. This rationale, this desperate grasp at a known devil over an unknown angel, is the only thing that sustains me.

But as the situation deteriorates further, I begin to question how long I can endure this existence.

My mother's voice echoes down the hallway, a series of desperate howls that chill the air between us as we approach. The scene that greets us as we enter the room is even more harrowing. My mother slams her body against the bars of a cage, her movements wild and uncontrolled. The floor is slick and wet—someone has recently sprayed her down, a dehumanizing method now routinely used instead of a bath. It doesn't get rid of the stench of urine and sweat and the underlying smell of decay. I'm sure my mother isn't the only inhabitant in the basement. I often hear the scurry of rats, yet I never seen them.

Walking over to a table lined with essentials, I pick up a handful of unwrapped protein bars and approach the cage cautiously. Sliding the bars through the gaps, I watch as my mother snatches them up, devouring them with the frantic energy of a starved animal. It's moments like this, watching the primal desperation, that I struggle to recognize her as the woman who raised me. She doesn't even bother to remove the wrappers; everything gets devoured like she can fill the void of hunger that isn't food related. I know that some part of her hunger for freedom will never happen. I've resigned myself to that fact that she will be caged forever.

Standing back, I fix my eyes on her, painfully aware of the maid's presence just a step behind me. The room fills with the harsh sounds of my mother's ragged eating, the silence between us stretching uncomfortably.

"It makes you think, doesn't it?" I finally say, my voice low, almost lost amidst the noise.

"What does, ma'am?" the maid replies, her tone neutral, perhaps cautiously curious.

"That all of us, underneath all of our upbringing and laws,

are this," I gesture toward my mother, her frenzied state a raw, unsettling exhibit of stripped humanity.

"I don't know if I agree with you there, ma'am," the maid responds, her tone cautious yet disagreeing.

"Oh, really? Hm." I lean in slightly, lowering my voice with a hint of venom. "It is interesting that, right before I arrived here, you were the one in Wolf's bed. And now, you are also the one who is actively making my life a living hell."

"This is a tough business, ma'am. Not everyone is made for it," she replies, her voice a blend of defensiveness and resignation.

"Bitch, this business was made for me." The words slip out, icy and sharp, as I reveal the gun strapped to my thigh and raise it to show the maid, who gasps, her eyes widening in shock.

I nod toward the cage. "Open the door."

The maid hesitates, fear flickering over her face, prompting me to fire a shot at her feet, causing her to jump and whimper, the dance of someone trying desperately to avoid being hurt. The noise shatters the calm inside me. The want to draw blood almost consumes me.

"Open the fucking door!" My voice is louder now, harsh and commanding. My heart races with excitement, and a sense of not belonging in my own skin tightens the flesh to my bones.

Tears stream down the maid's face as she begs, "Please, be merciful."

I step closer, flashing a coy, cute smile that masks the brewing storm within me. Grabbing her by the hair as roughly as Wolf has grabbed mine, I draw her close, my voice mocking, "This is a tough business, ma'am."

With a forceful shove, I push her into the cage and swiftly lock the door behind her. My mother, driven mad by whatever chemicals course through her veins, drops the protein bars and lunges at the new prey trapped with her.

My mother's dig into the maid's face is fast and animalistic. The maid tries to cover her face, but she is no match for my mother's insanity. I want to stay and watch, but I'm also aware I fired a gun, and the noise may attract Wolf. A plan had already formed in my mind, stating that the maid had hidden a gun and fired a shot at me as I fed my mother. I had wrestled the gun away and pushed the maid into the cage in a frantic plea to get away. I smile.

As I step away from the cage, the maid's screams join my mother's, filling the corridor with a chilling duet of terror. Walking down the hallway, the reality of what I've done sets in. But around me, silence reigns—no one dares complain or intervene. In this twisted world of Wolf's creation, I've just rewritten the rules, proving that I can play this game just as ruthlessly.

CHAPTER THIRTEEN

Diarmuid

The Church, the bar where men like me convene, welcomes me with the scent of stale beer and old smoke that clings to my clothes instantly.

Lorcan's outside one of the private booths when I spot him. He's leaning against the wall, an impatient smirk playing on his lips as he catches sight of me. He jerks his head, motioning me to follow. The bass from the speakers makes the floor thrum under my feet as we navigate through clusters of drunken revelers.

We push through the velvet curtain into a dimly lit alcove. Ronan is there, the center of a scene that's more steamy than stylish. A dancer straddles him, her movements slow and purposeful, barely clothed and less concerned with dancing than with the man beneath her. Ronan's hands are a mix of tenderness and possession as he traces the curve of her spine, his lips worshiping the exposed skin of her chest.

The moment fractures when Lorcan whistles sharply. Heads turn, and the music seems to fade into the background. Ronan looks up, annoyance flashing in his eyes before he resettles them into a kind of resigned mischief.

"You were supposed to keep watch until I was finished," Ronan says, his voice a blend of jest and jab.

"We don't have that much time, brother," Lorcan replies, glancing at his watch with exaggerated attention.

Ronan gives the dancer one last, deep kiss that seems to speak volumes about endings. With a practiced ease, he eases her off his lap. A playful smack on her rear sends her on her way, a flirty giggle echoing behind her. He fixes his clothes with quick fingers, his gaze lifting to meet mine as he buckles his belt. His all-too-familiar grin, spreads across his face.

"Jealous?" he teases, his eyebrow arching in challenge.

"Not at all," I shoot back, my tone flat.

"Why should Diarmuid be jealous? He has two beautiful brides waiting for him at home," Lorcan quips, a smirk dancing on his lips as he leans out of the booth, catching the eye of a passing server with a snap of his fingers. He murmurs our drink order before ducking back into our secluded spot, the velvet curtain swaying slightly at his movement.

The three of us gather around the small, dimly lit table. The air is thick with the residue of earlier indulgences and the underlying tension that seems to follow Ronan and me like a shadow.

"You lost your Bride to Wolf. That is a kick to the balls," Ronan throws at me, his voice low but edged with a kind of cruel amusement.

"Wolf was given something I no longer wanted," I respond calmly, though the muscles in my jaw tighten just enough to betray my irritation.

"After he had already sampled it," Ronan adds, a smirk pulling at his mouth, his eyes glinting with provocation.

The air between us crackles, every word laden with old grudges and unspoken grievances. Lorcan senses the rising tension—he always does—andexcuses himself. I glare at Ronan.

"Your shirt is hanging out," I say.

He glances down and starts to tuck it in.

Lorcan returns moments later with three glasses, each filled with a dark liquid. He sets them down with a precision that feels more like a peace offering than a simple gesture of hospitality.

"Look, both of you need to keep your dicks away and your mouths shut because I have news," Lorcan begins, his tone a mix of irritation and seriousness. We both quiet, turning our attention to him. "As you know, Tyrone Lynch is our new Taoiseach, which leaves his ministry position completely open for the taking. The President is favoring me for Minister of Justice."

The significance of his words sinks in. For the Hand of Kings, Lorcan's potential appointment is a monumental advantage, a strategic position that could sway political currents in our favor.

For our family, it's a badge of honor, a step towards solidifying the O'Sullivan name in the annals of power.

Ronan is the first to break into a grin, clapping Lorcan on the back. "That's brilliant, brother! Minister of Justice, eh? Who would've thought?"

I echo the congratulations, my words coated in a veneer of pride and support. "That's a great achievement, Lorcan. Truly."

But inside, a storm brews. It's not just about the position or the power. It's the ease with which my brothers seem to navigate these waters, while I find myself continually caught in the undertow of their successes and my own missteps.

Lorcan, holding his drink like a judge about to pronounce a sentence, turns his gaze toward me. His expression is somber, as if he's weighing the cost of every word before he speaks. "This means that we need to be more careful than we've ever been in our family's history." He pauses, taking a measured sip, his eyes never leaving mine. "Now, Ronan, I'm not too worried about you. All of your shit is still legal, right?"

Ronan laughs, a sound full of mirth and carelessness. "Well, legal enough that the authorities won't do anything. All palms have been properly greased."

"Excellent." Lorcan nods, apparently satisfied, but the air shifts as his focus tightens on me. "The only problem that I may have is you." His tone is flat, almost regretful, yet there's an edge to it—a sharpness meant to cut through any pretense.

Ronan's grin broadens, reveling in the drama, his earlier

jests forgotten as he senses the tide turning in a direction he finds immensely entertaining.

"Me, brother?" I respond, keeping my voice even, masking the surge of frustration boiling inside. I take a slow sip of my drink, letting the cool liquid temper the heat of my emotions. I need to tread carefully; this conversation could define much more than my role in the family—it could determine my very path forward.

Lorcan sets his glass down with a precision that mirrors his intent. "Yes, you. Your... ventures have always skirted the edge of what's permissible. And with this new position, if I take it, the spotlight won't just be on me. It will be on all of us, on every move we make. Any slip from you could not only undermine my position but could bring the whole family down."

I nod slowly, the weight of his words not lost on me. The room feels colder, the shadows darker. "I understand the stakes, Lorcan," I say, my voice steady despite the turmoil inside. "You'll have no trouble from me. I'll keep my affairs in order."

Lorcan studies me for a moment longer, as if searching for any sign of deceit. Finally, he nods, apparently satisfied with my assurance. "I need more than just words, Diarmuid. I need actions. Prove to me—and to the family—that you can handle this. That you're not just another liability."

Ronan's smirk fades into a more contemplative expression as he watches our exchange. He knows as well as I do that this isn't just about legality or maintaining a facade; it's about survival, about the delicate balance we maintain in a world that's always one step away from chaos.

As the conversation drifts towards other matters—plans and precautions, strategies and safeguards—I find myself more isolated than ever. The path I've chosen, the one that leads away from the darkness of the cult that has ensnared my family, seems lonelier and fraught with danger. Lorcan's potential ascent within the cult's political arm isn't just a complication; it's a direct challenge to everything I hope to achieve.

The night winds down with empty glasses and hollow laughter. Lorcan and I part ways with Ronann and backslaps that promise to stay aligned, but as I step out into the night, the cool air feels like a balm. I'm left with a resolve hardened by the evening's revelations. Convincing Lorcan to turn away from the allure of power the cult offers won't be easy, but necessary. My plans, my hopes for our family's future depend on it. And as I walk away from the bar, the shadows no longer feel like just concealment for my thoughts—they feel like the companions of my resolve.

"Yes. Your arms dealing. Your situation with your Brides. The fallout of Uncle Andrew's murder. All of the shit hitting the fan needs to be redirected elsewhere. This is our family's chance. We cannot be caught, or it may take another hundred years to get someone in this position again. But it's not just you. It's Wolf," Lorcan says.

Wolf. The name alone is enough to bring a scowl to my face. Once a Duke, now a Marquess. "Wolf is a ticking time bomb," Lorcan continues, echoing the reports from our spies. "According to the spy we have in Wolf's residence, he has finally been broken—but it isn't the kind of broken that leads to timidness."

"What do you suggest we do?" I ask, the frustration evident in my voice. "Before the Kings, the family could decide to remove someone like Wolf. Now, he has a rank. We are not allowed to interfere in any potential plans that Victor has for him."

"We need to find a way to reassure him that someone gives a fuck about what happened to Uncle Andrew," Lorcan asserts, his eyes scanning our faces for any sign of dissent.

That someone isn't me.

"I am becoming the Minister of Justice," Lorcan adds, a hint of resolve in his tone. "I will have more useful contacts now. We can try to use my resources to find his killer."

"And Sofia Hughes's killer," I interject, dropping another name into the conversation, one that hasn't come up tonight but haunts me nonetheless.

"Who?" Lorcan asks.

"Sofia Hughes," I state firmly, making sure they understand the gravity of the name. "It was her murder that led to the authorities even finding Uncle Andrew's body. Whoever left her there knows who killed Uncle Andrew."

There's a heavy pause. The implication hangs in the air, thick and accusatory. And beneath that, a silent fear courses through me—the fear of exposure.

Hopefully, I can get to that person before they tell the world that I was the one who killed my uncle.

Lorcan nods slowly, his gaze sharp. "I can look into this, Diarmuid. Until then, keep your noses clean. Both of you." His voice is firm, commanding—a leader's voice, preparing for battle.

The conversation shifts as the night wears on, transitioning into lighter topics, perhaps as a way to cleanse the palate from the earlier heaviness. We talk of sports, of local news, of trivial matters that don't sear the soul. But even as laughter fills the gaps, my mind doesn't stray far from the shadows.

When I finally make my way home, the cool night air feels like a cloak, wrapping around me, hiding my thoughts from the world. I mull over my promises, the ones made to my Brides. Selene's discovery of the medallion looms large in my thoughts. She believes it holds the key to much more than just historical curiosity—it might be a doorway to answers, to freedom.

Whatever that medallion is, I doubt it will lead me to a place free of trouble. I realize it doesn't matter. The promise of freedom, of escape from the binds of this life, is worth any peril.

Freedom is always worth it.

CHAPTER FOURTEEN

Niamh

I am losing. The realization slices through me, a cold, sharp truth I can no longer deny. I can feel it, not just in the depths of my crumbling heart but etched into the very marrow of my bones. It's in Diarmuid's touch—automatic, detached—a stark contrast to the slower, more tender caresses he reserves for Selene. Despite my deep affection for her, this is a contest. Brutal and unequivocal. Only one of us will ascend as his Consort, and the fate of the one who doesn't—unthinkable, yet terrifyingly possible.

Amira had told us about our potential futures, her voice dripping with a venomous glee. She spoke of discarded Brides of Kings, passed down like unwanted heirlooms from Dukes to Marquesses, or worse, delivered directly into the clutches of Wolf.

Whether her tales are woven from truth or lies, the possibility ignites a primal fear within me, conjuring visions of faceless, cruel men waiting like vultures for their chance to strike.

I stand on the balcony, the chill of the early morning air biting through the thick fabric of my housecoat. Wrapped tightly around me, it's a small barrier against the cold and the ever-watchful eyes of the guards patrolling below. The memory of Selene, gracelessly caught as she attempted to shimmy down into the freedom of the backyard, flashes in my mind. That escape route is firmly closed now, sealed by Diarmuid's tightened security measures.

I sip my tea, its warmth a fleeting comfort. Diarmuid insists that being shadowed by guards is normal in this life of opulence and hidden dangers. Yet, he bristles at the thought of his Brides— his possessions—being followed too closely. A part of me kindles hope at this protective streak, interpreting it as care. But then, the more cynical voice in my head scoffs, to Diarmuid, we are merely things he owns, not individuals he cherishes. He is not the type to share his toys, only to safeguard them to assert his control.

With a sigh, I step back from the railing, leaving the cool outside for the plush warmth of the interior. The carpet feels indulgent beneath my bare feet, a stark contrast to the unforgiving cold of the balcony's stone. Our bedroom, shared by Diarmuid, Selene, and me, feels too large and yet suffocatingly small at the same time. It's a gilded cage with silken linens.

I wander toward Selene's room, where everything we took from her apartment is displayed. . As I pass by the vacant room intended for Amira, unease curls in my stomach.

What do we do with such a room?

I push open the door, the familiar creak soft in the quiet hall, and find Selene exactly where I expect her to be. She's hunched over her laptop, her focus absolute as her fingers dance across the keyboard. The room around her is a chaotic reflection of our collective mission—a recreation of her old apartment's setup but intensified. Print-outs, photos, and strings crisscross the walls, creating a visual web of our investigations. The room smells faintly of her perfume, a floral scent that now seems as much a part of her as her rebellious streak. I wonder if that's why Diarmuid seems to favor her more—her defiant nature?

"Anything new?" I ask, stepping inside and closing the door behind me gently.

Selene looks up, her eyes briefly flitting to the digital chaos before settling on me. "Maybe," she murmurs, a note of cautious optimism in her voice. "It's like putting together a puzzle with half the pieces missing."

I move closer, glancing over her shoulder at the screen. The display shows a complex diagram of connections, centering on a photo of Amira's brother, Michael. Diarmuid had added it himself, pinning it prominently on our makeshift investigation board. His involvement had been unexpectedly beneficial. With his background in the O'Sullivan mafia and deeper ties into cult activities, he had managed to quash numerous false leads that could have derailed us.

Yet, despite Diarmuid's extensive network, gaps remain, the answers frustratingly out of reach. He knows a lot, yet not as much as Victor, the enigmatic leader who seems to hold all the cards. "Diarmuid really thinks Michael is key to getting closer to Victor?" I question, skepticism threading through my tone.

Selene nods, pushing back a stray lock of hair that had escaped her ponytail. "He does. Michael's both the mouthpiece and the earpiece for Victor. If we can get to him, convince him somehow..."

Her voice trails off, the implication hanging between us. It would be a dangerous game approaching Michael. Diarmuid had made it clear that any attempt to engage with him would need meticulous planning. Michael was not just a spokesperson; he was a sentinel, acutely aware of any threats to Victor or their clandestine operations.

I trace my finger along the edge of the photograph of Sofia Hughes, pinned carefully amidst a sea of other images and notes. There's something about Sofia that resonates deeply with me, something beyond the scope of this investigation. Perhaps it's because I see shades of my own little sister in her—the same defiant spark, the same stubborn tilt of the chin. Maura, Sofia's sister, and the fierce love she couldn't show before it was too late, haunts me. I often wonder, lying awake at night, about the final moments of Sofia's life. Who was it that ended her dreams, snuffed out her light? Did she call out to Maura with her last breath?

Beside me, Selene's focus never wavers from her screen, her eyes flicking back and forth as she absorbs the influx of digital information. Her approach to this entire ordeal is precise, almost clinical, a stark contrast to the emotional storm that rages inside me. For Selene, Sofia is a case to be solved, a piece in a complex puzzle of corruption and hidden agendas. She acknowledges the tragedy but remains detached, finding a necessary distance that I find myself unable to maintain.

Selene's latest discovery that Sofia had connections within the government has only fueled her fervor. She pores over online archives, pulling up photographs of Cóisir Amárach's public engagements, which is the newest political party in Ireland. "Look at this," Selene suddenly calls out, her voice pulling me back from my thoughts.

I move closer, peering over her shoulder at her laptop screen. She points at a photograph from a ribbon-cutting ceremony, where Sofia can be seen in the background, her expression unreadable. "She's everywhere Cóisir Amárach was," Selene notes, her tone laced with intrigue. "It's like she was shadowing them, or maybe it was the other way around."

I nod, though my thoughts linger on the photo I was just examining—the one of Sofia at the National Museum of Ireland. In it, she leans casually against a pillar, looking out of place yet entirely at ease, as if she knows secrets about the people and the stones around her. Beside her, Tyrone Lynch, a known associate of Cóisir Amárach, engages animatedly with the museum curator.

"I think we need to visit the museum," I say.

"Why?" Selene asks, turning to me.

"I can't explain it, Selene," I say, frustration coloring my voice. "But ever since we saw that photo of Sofia and Tyrone Lynch at the museum, something doesn't sit right with me. We might find something there, something everyone else has overlooked."

Selene sighs, her expression softening slightly as she recognizes my determination. "Fine." She relents, but not without a pointed look. "But if we're going down this rabbit hole, we're doing it thoroughly."

She reaches for the medallion lying amidst the scattered papers on the desk. She turns it over in her hands thoughtfully before slipping it into her pocket. Her obsession with decoding its secrets has grown with every dead end we've hit; it's as if she believes the medallion itself holds the answers to our sprawling investigation.

"Let me get changed." I quickly return to the room and throw on some jeans and a sweater. This will take my mind off this competition and give me something productive to do.

Together, we descend the stairs to the foyer, where one of Diarmuid's men is stationed by the door. His presence is both a reassurance and a reminder of the constant surveillance we live under.

"Where to today?" he asks, his voice betraying no interest beyond professional courtesy.

"The National Museum of Ireland," I reply, meeting his gaze steadily. The mention of the museum doesn't raise an eyebrow; he's used to our sudden outings by now, though the destinations are rarely this cultural.

He nods, reaching for his radio to call in the car. As we wait, I can't shake the feeling that we're stepping closer to a hidden truth.

As we pull up to the National Museum of Ireland, I can't help but feel a surge of both excitement and trepidation. The grandeur of the building's archaeology strikes me immediately—it's majestic, standing confidently among Dublin's historic architecture. Even though I've wandered through many of Europe's grand opera houses and theaters, the museum's imposing facade and the elegance of its structure demand a moment of admiration.

"I've never been to this part of the museum," I say as we step out of the car, my eyes scanning the elaborate stonework and towering columns.

Selene gives me a brief smile, her mind clearly elsewhere. "Let's hope it's worth the trip," she says, adjusting the strap of her bag over her shoulder.

We pass through the security checks, and the tightness of the measures reminds me that whatever secret Diarmuid is keeping from us must be more significant than just familial scandals and tragic deaths. There's an undercurrent of something larger at play, something potentially dangerous.

Inside, the museum is relatively quiet, a typical weekday scene with a few groups of tourists milling about. The sound of a primary school group echoes faintly from another gallery, their young voices a stark contrast to the otherwise solemn atmosphere. I watch them for a moment as they're led around by a teacher, their curiosity unbounded as they point at displays and artifacts.

Selene and I head toward the main room, where the gold artifacts are displayed. My gaze sweeps over the items, each piece telling a story of Ireland's rich and tumultuous history. While

Selene seems to recognize some of the pieces, likely from her extensive readings, I am seeing most of them for the first time. Growing up, history lessons in my house were more focused on the tragic lives of famed ballerinas than on national heritage.

"These pieces are incredible, aren't they?" I say to Selene, drawn to a display of ancient gold necklaces and brooches. Their craftsmanship is exquisite, a testament to the skill and artistry of their makers.

My childhood studies, the dramatic, often tragic stories of ballerinas like Mathilde Kschessinska, Emma Livry, and Heidi Guenther were my history lessons—women whose lives were as glittering and as fragile as the delicate pieces before me. Their struggles with power, fate, and vulnerability resonate deeply as I trace the contours of a golden torc, imagining it as a halo once worn by those ill-fated dancers.

A great golden shield captures my reflection, and for a moment, I'm not just a visitor in a museum; I am part of this collection, another story of potential and peril. The shield throws back an image of myself: Niamh Connolly, twenty-two, once a ballerina, now a Bride of Diarmuid O'Sullivan. The uncertainty of my future weighs heavily as I move away from the shield, the reflection distorted as the angle changes.

Drawn inexplicably toward a familiar pillar, a sense of déjà vu washes over me. I can almost see Sofia Hughes, her presence as palpable as if she were standing before me, urging me toward this very spot. I leave Selene engrossed in her examination of a collection of decorative spears and approach the pillar.

Beside it, a new exhibit catches my eye—a collection on loan from the British Museum featuring relics once belonging to John Dee, the famed Elizabethan alchemist and occultist. Among these is a piece that immediately draws me in: a flat, thin slab of obsidian, polished to a dark, ominous sheen. The label beside it identifies it as an Aztec mirror used by John Dee to conjure demons. Its surface is so finely polished that, despite its dark color, it reflects my face with an unsettling clarity.

The revelation sends a chill down my spine. It reveals Enochian—the language of the angels, as Dee claimed. I look at the medallion in Selene's hand, its inscriptions suddenly not just mere markings but potentially a language of celestial power, according to one of history's most infamous mystics. It's all too much to absorb in the quiet hum of the museum gallery.

"Are you saying this..." I gesture to the medallion, "...could be something more than just a decorative artifact?" My voice is tinged with a mixture of skepticism and wonder.

Selene looks up from her phone, her brow furrowed. "I don't know what to think anymore, Niamh. This is way out of my depth." She pauses, considering the weight of her next words. "But if this medallion and these relics share the same script, there has to be a connection. Maybe Sofia stumbled upon it, too."

I glance back at the pillar, the silent stone sentinel that seems to stand as a gateway to deeper mysteries. Sofia had leaned against this very pillar, possibly contemplating the same enigmatic connections that now lay before us. What had she known? What had she uncovered that might have led to her untimely demise?

"Selene, what if this isn't just about political games or the mafia? What if Sofia was onto something... bigger?" The words feel absurd as they escape my lips, but the day's discoveries have been anything but ordinary.

Selene shakes her head, a gesture not of denial but of dawning realization. "We need to dig deeper into this. Enochian, John Dee, these artifacts... there's a story here, one that no one has pieced together yet." She snaps a few photos of the tablets and the medallion, her mind already racing through the implications.

I nod, my thoughts swirling. Magic doesn't exist in the world as I was taught to understand it, a world of clear rules and tangible truths. Yet, here in the shadows of history, surrounded by relics of a man who believed he could speak with angels, I can't help but feel that some mysteries defy clear explanations.

As Selene dives deeper into her phone, scouring the internet for every scrap of information on Enochian and its mysteries, I stand there, between the echoes of the past and the whispers of something inexplicable. This journey started with Sofia, but now it stretches into realms neither of us could have anticipated. My heart races as I realize that this investigation might change everything I thought I knew about the world.

"Let's take everything we've found here and go over it tonight," I suggest, my voice steady despite the turmoil inside. "Every detail could be crucial."

Selene nods, snapping out of her digital dive. "Yes, let's do that. We're in this deep, might as well see where it leads."

We leave the museum with more questions than answers, the

weight of the unknown pressing heavily upon us. But within me, a flame of curiosity is kindled, fueled by the possibility that in this vast, mysterious universe, there are indeed things that cannot be fully explained. And perhaps, just perhaps, we are on the verge of uncovering one of them.

CHAPTER FIFTEEN

Diarmuid

The sharp bite of winter dances along my hands as I push open the wrought-iron gate of St. Gertrude's private courtyard garden. It's a sanctuary, not just for prayer but for decisions darker than the clergy would endorse. The notice that flipped today's agenda on its head had come by courier just hours after I checked in at the Silent Prince, my usual haunt when matters in Dublin call me back from my less publicized endeavors.

Some brazen mafia family from Limerick, new players on the scene, decided it was their turn to try selling arms in my Dublin. My men, fiercely loyal hounds, were ready to tear through the streets and launch a full-scale assault on these would-be invaders.

But those days of immediate bloodshed are relics—or at least, they're supposed to be. We plan, we cover up, we strategize.

The messages we sent back were cold, hostile in their politeness. "Dublin is not open for new business," they read, a warning wrapped in formality. Deals were put on the table, but nothing that would lose us territory. The O'Sullivans hadn't ceded ground in three generations; this wasn't going to be the day that changed.

"They are testing the waters," Allen had murmured earlier, his eyes scanning the lines of text for anything we might have missed. "Without a named, official head of the O'Sullivan family, they think they can encroach on your territory."

Walking through the sanctuary now, past the empty pews that echo with hollow promises of redemption, I can't help but scoff. I've been here, on my knees, praying to a god who never seemed to listen, not when bullets tore through my flesh, not when my own blood pooled around me, slick and accusing.

If God won't save you, then you damn well must make yourself a King.

Usually, when I return to my sanctuary, the presence of my two Brides were enough to shrink any problem to a manageable size. When I walked back from the Silent Prince with this in mind, though, that didn't happen. The courier's sudden appearance, hastily remounting his bicycle, snapped me back into the moment. I flicked my fingers—a simple gesture he recognized immediately. He scrambled over, slightly breathless as he handed me the message.

No words, just a symbol—a hand with a crown in the palm. The message was clear. I had been summoned. That's what led me to St. Gertrude's.

Inside, the sanctuary is quiet except for the hum of a vacuum cleaner. A woman, her back to me, works diligently over the carpet. She senses my presence, straightening up to look at me before nodding toward the left side of the sanctuary. That gesture, simple and direct, tells me all I need to know about where I need to go next. I nod in thanks, my mind already racing through the possibilities of what awaits.

To my left, the stained-glass windows cast colorful patterns on the stone floor, light streaming through scenes of biblical triumphs and tragedies, a reminder of the eternal battles between good and evil. I turn right instead, heading for a less conspicuous part of the church.

The hallway is quieter, the sacred murals and the smell of old wood filling the air as I move toward the offices and the rectory beyond. But my destination is nearer; a discreet door to the right, leading to the private courtyard.

As I step through the doorway, I'm met with the sight of two figures, their forms draped in robes, ostensibly busy dusting the decorative sconces that line the walls. To an untrained eye, they appear simply as part of the church's staff, blending seamlessly into the background of this sacred place. But I know better. The subtle way the fabric of their robes shifts reveals all I need to know—slits at the waist, cleverly concealed, designed for quick access to hidden weapons. They don't acknowledge my presence, but I sense their awareness like a tangible thing in the air.

In the private courtyard, the ambiance shifts starkly. The lush greens of summer have surrendered to the browns and blacks of the impending November, a stark reminder of the seasons changing, much like the loyalties of men. It's too late in the year for planting or pruning; yet there's activity here, misplaced and telling.

Victor Madigan bends intently over some flowering bushes protected by a tarp, his fingers working soil that hasn't yet succumbed to winter's chill. Around him, others mimic his actions, but their awkward movements betray them. They aren't gardeners any more than those figures were mere cleaners.

Victor doesn't rise or even turn at my approach. His back to me, the vulnerability of his exposed neck is almost inviting. My gaze lingers there briefly before drifting to the assortment of gardening tools scattered carelessly by his side—a collection of potential weapons or tools for burial.

The thought flits across my mind with disturbing ease—a fleeting, dark whisper that I could end it all right here. How simple it would be to pick up a spade, the heft of it reassuring in my grip, and step forward—just a few paces, a swift, silent stride, and then a quick, forceful motion. A life could be snuffed out just beneath these sacred arches.

The vivid image unfolds in my head: the sharp, clean plunge into the back of Victor's neck, severing the spinal cord, rendering him helpless as his brain screams commands into a void of unresponsive nerves. The horror in his eyes, wide and uncomprehending, as his body betrays him. Then, with a cold precision, the violent crushing of bone under heel, a gruesome punctuation to a silent exclamation.

I shudder, pushing the thought away as quickly as it comes. If such thoughts were visible, if the people around me could glimpse the shadowed corners of my mind, I'd be dead. Dead and buried right here in this garden. Come spring, flowers would bloom over my grave, a riot of color fed by my decay, as Victor parades his next protégé through this garden of death.

Victor's voice pulls me back from these dark musings. He bends down, picking up a hand trowel and working at something buried in the soil, his back still vulnerably turned to me. "Too many people assume gardens only need tending when they are beautiful," he says, his voice light, almost contemplative.

Being Victor's personal hitman isn't something I broadcast. Not even my brothers, who think they know all my secrets, are aware of this particular role I play.

I rub the back of my neck, feeling the tension knotting there. Victor complicates everything. When I was a child, he and my uncle made sure I knew what Hell felt like. I managed to get my revenge on my uncle, but Victor... he's another story. There's a part of me, dark and twisted, that wants to end him. But then there's this other part, equally dark yet different—it craves the violence, the release that comes with each hit. Victor fuels that part, gives it what it needs to survive.

Victor rises and claps his hands, sending clods of earth scattering to the ground. His movements are deliberate, almost theatrical. He knows I'm watching every motion, calculating, always calculating. He's aware of the thread that tethers my loyalty to him—a thread worn thin by the years of manipulation and pain he orchestrated. Yet, here he stands, seemingly at ease in the twilight of this garden, discussing history as if we were mere acquaintances discussing the weather.

He points toward a corner of the garden where two trees stand intertwined. One, gnarled and ancient, seems almost protective of the younger, healthier one embracing it. The symbolism isn't lost on me; it's Victor's way of storytelling, always layered with meaning, always a lesson.

"Three hundred years ago," he begins, his voice steady and clear, "a priest by the name of Giolla na Naomh planted that tree in remembrance of the martyrdom of his mentor, Laoiseac of the Eventide. Laoiseach was not made a saint, mind you. He sacrificed his life with no real purpose or vision. His death meant nothing to anyone but his student. That tree has been growing in that corner since Giolla na Naomh became the priest of this parish. If it wasn't for my own interest in historical records, no one living would know who planted that tree."

He pauses, his eyes locking onto mine as he turns his hand slightly, his fingers directed at the younger tree. His gaze is probing, as if he's using the tale of the trees to gauge my reaction, to see if I understand the lesson he's imparting.

"The day I became the keeper of this garden, I planted that tree right against Giolla na Noamh's tree," Victor continues, his voice almost reflective as he gazes at the entwined trees. "Now, after all these years, the older tree is failing as the younger tree is competing for its resources."

He turns to face me, those cold, unfeeling eyes locking onto mine—eyes that haven't changed since I was just a boy under his heavy hand. I remember the way the candlelight flickered across his face during those endless nights in the chapel, casting shadows that seemed to devour any hint of warmth or kindness. The light never did reach the dark recesses of his eyes, places where no warmth could possibly dwell.

Memories surge, unbidden. The searing pain as my tiny hand was forced against the flame, the cruel snap of the whip across my back whenever I dared to pull away. Each memory is a blade, each moment a lingering echo of pain. But outwardly, I remain unchanged, a mask of calm connectedness firmly in place. Victor molded me into this—into someone who could endure, who could suppress, and survive.

"I expected the new tree to push aside the old." Victor's voice is a low murmur, barely stirring the air. The little wind that manages to slip into the courtyard seems to snatch his words, whisking them away before they can fully sink in. But I catch them, every syllable, even as they drift toward oblivion.

His gaze stays locked onto mine, hard and unyielding. The metaphor sheds its disguise, and the meaning behind his words crystallizes. He's no longer talking about trees—he's talking about me, Diarmuid, the young tree he carefully planted.

And Oisin, the older tree I had destroyed. The name alone conjures a storm within me: Oisin, the whisper in the dark, the ghost story for unruly children. Yet, to me, he was something else entirely—a protector, perhaps the only adult who never raised a hand against me. It's a strange irony to be more cherished by a known killer than by your own flesh and blood.

But Victor had other plans. He sent Oisin after Niamh and Selene, a mission from which he never returned. And I, the dutiful instrument of Victor's will, ensured it.

Victor bends over, his hands busy in the soil, attending to a task. My gaze fixes on the vulnerable nape of his neck, and my hand twitches almost imperceptibly at my side. The old urge, the deep-seated need for action, flares up.

"He was of use to you," I say, my voice steady, masking the turmoil underneath.

"Until he wasn't," Victor replies without looking up, his attention still on his gardening.

"You sent him," I push, needing him to acknowledge it, to voice the betrayal.

"And you stopped him," he returns simply, straightening up to look at me again. There's a flicker of something—approval, perhaps, or the acknowledgment of my role in his grand design. "If you were anything but a King, you wouldn't be breathing right now, Diarmuid. I must respect your decisions as much as you respect mine. Lord knows we have a long history of disappointing each other." His voice is tinged with a cold formality, as if he's merely discussing the weather rather than our tangled, violent history.

So that's how he sees it—disappointments. All those years

of manipulation and torment, reduced to mere disappointments in his eyes.

"There is one thing that must be corrected, however." Victor's voice pulls me back from the edge of my brooding thoughts. He sweeps his hand over the soil, uncovering a thick, gnarled root that snakes around the smaller, more fragile roots of the nearby tarp-covered flower bushes. He whistles sharply, a signal that brings others in the garden forward. They clutch tools and move toward the bushes with determined strides.

My muscles tense, every nerve on high alert. For a moment, I'm convinced this is it—this is where my story ends, in the very garden that bore witness to so many of Victor's twisted lessons. Instinctively, my hand drifts to my gun, but Victor's touch stops me. His fingers are light on my arm, almost reassuring, as he guides me away from the scene.

"Japanese knotweed. Very invasive," he explains, his tone now almost conversational. "All of my careful planning within these walls is being destroyed by the growth of something that does not belong."

Victor's voice drops to a murmur, laden with a dangerous edge, as he leans in close. His eyes harden, the threat manifesting in the intensity of his gaze, leaving no room for ambiguity.

"Your Brides infiltrated my Page's office during the Harvest Moon ceremony. They have also been poking around places they should not be." His voice is a hiss, each word a pointed dagger aimed directly at me. "Control them, Diarmuid, or…"

He lets the sentence hang ominously in the air, turning his

head slightly to gaze out at the garden workers. I follow his gaze, watching as they aggressively rip the invasive vine from the soil, their tools chopping and tearing it into pieces with ruthless efficiency.

".. your garden will be weeded," Victor concludes, his voice cold, a stark contrast to the violence of the scene unfolding in front of us. His message couldn't be clearer. The consequences of failing to rein in my Brides are spelled out in the fate of the unwanted vines—cut down, torn apart, utterly destroyed.

Victor claps me on the shoulder, a gesture that feels more like a warning than a reassurance. He then turns away, walking back toward the chaos of the vine removal, leaving me to digest the severity of his words.

When Kings Bend

CHAPTER SIXTEEN

Amira

I grip the blade tightly, feeling its cool, unforgiving edge. As I draw it across the girl's belly, a perfect line of blood beads up in its wake—not too deep, not too shallow. The dim light catches the metallic sheen, and I carefully guide the weapon to a new spot along her skin, pressing just enough to maintain the delicate flow.

"Stop. That's enough. Get cleaned up," I command, my voice echoing slightly in the sparsely furnished room. This place, reserved for the ones not quite adept enough with their hands, mouths, or other more intimate talents, is designed for pain—either giving or receiving. The beds are stark, clad in hospital-grade sheets, and the floors are bare, hard, and cold, stained with countless drops of blood.

I glance around, my gaze lingering on the door for a moment. Beyond it, rooms hold horrors that most can't fathom. But for me, the real terror has shifted—it's no longer just the Pain Room. It's Wolf's bedroom that haunts my thoughts now.

The makeup on my face feels thick, plastered over every visible inch of skin to cover the bruises and the secrets beneath. My collars ride high, and my sleeves stretch long down my arms, hiding more than just flesh.

Lately, I've been taking the drugs Wolf pushes at me. It's easier that way. Pain, after all, is only real when you're sober.

The girl in front of me is barely a woman, her body marked by shallow curves and a childish fullness in her cheeks. Once, curiosity got the better of me, and I dared ask Wolf if any of our "cargo" were minors. His response was a beer bottle hurled at my head.

She takes the towel I offer, dabbing at the blood on her stomach with shaky hands. Wolf's voice suddenly bellows from his corner, a deep, grating sound that used to make me flinch. But not anymore. I stand still, unaffected, and I can feel his anger boiling over. It infuriates him that I no longer react, that I don't show fear. He thrives on the fear of others, sees it as a tribute to his power. But my defiance seems like a personal affront, a challenge to his authority.

As I watch the girl clean herself, a part of me wonders just how much more of this life I can stand. How much longer can I wear this mask, dance to Wolf's twisted tunes? But then, what choice do I have? This isn't just about survival anymore. It's about revenge.

"I saved you," he constantly reminds me, his voice dripping with a twisted sense of benevolence. I don't look at him, don't give him the satisfaction of seeing my response.

Wolf thumps on the wall twice with his fist, a signal I've become familiar with. A hidden door swings open, and two young women step out, their eyes wide, uncertain. "Not you," he growls, pointing at the redhead who hesitates, then steps back. "Her." His finger shifts to the other girl, one with brown hair, much like my own.

It's a cruel tactic, a new game he's devised. He's been choosing girls that look like me, as if to replace or replicate me. A few days ago, it was a woman with warm brown eyes—eyes that mirrored mine before he had them blinded. His actions are a message, a warning of what he could do to me.

Now, in this stark room, he instructs the chosen girl to lie down beside the one still trembling from her own cuts. "Cut her," he commands the bleeding girl.

"She hasn't been trained yet to do it to others," I intervene quietly, watching the new girl's chest rise and fall rapidly with fear.

"That's what I'm doing," Wolf snaps back, dismissive, his patience wearing thin. I glance at him, taking in the signs of his recent indulgence. The dried blood inside his nostrils isn't from a fight—it's from his latest binge on cocaine. The drug makes him even more unpredictable, less human.

Wolf barks at the girls, his voice sharp and unforgiving. "Do it!" he commands the bleeding girl, pointing at the one who looks like me. As she starts to cry, Wolf is upon her in a flash, his hand raised, striking her face repeatedly.

Without thinking, I lunge forward and grab his arm, stopping him mid-swing. Time seems to freeze as he turns his furious gaze on me. I know I've crossed a line. Panic seizes me, but my survival instincts kick in. With nowhere to run, I press my lips to his in a desperate act of diversion.

My heart races as I use every trick I've learned to keep his attention on me, giving the other girls a sliver of a chance to escape the room. It's a grim dance, far from the violence of that day in the hallway, yet devoid of any real affection. My clothes take the brunt of his rough hands. He doesn't bother undressing, only bends me over a bed and attacks me from behind. I moan at the right time, not wanting to anger him. As he pumps viciously into me, I tighten my eyes, and my moans are released through gritted teeth. When he slams into me and cries out his own release, I do the same, pretending that I'm not sore, pretending that I don't feel like a disgusting creature. Instead, when he pulls out of me, I glance over my shoulder and offer him a sweet smile.

He smiles back and pulls me onto the closest bed that still has stains of blood beneath us. He doesn't seem to notice.

As we lie side by side, Wolf kisses my hands gently, as if we are lovers basking in the afterglow. "You are so good at this," he murmurs, his voice soft.

"Only with you," I reply, my voice steady despite the turmoil inside. I say what he wants to hear, inflating his ego, making him feel revered. It's a dangerous game, but it's one that keeps me marginally safer.

Lying there, Wolf's expression turns distant as he stares at the ceiling, lost in memories. He begins to speak of his father, how he was brutally killed, his bones broken long before his death. "Andrew O'Sullivan was a King in the order," he says, his voice tinged with a mix of reverence and pain. "They should have torn the world apart to find his killer."

"And they haven't," Wolf muses aloud, his voice turning cold. "That means the command had to come from the top. From Victor." His words hang in the air, a dangerous implication that could seal our fates.

This is insane, I think to myself. As much as I try to play my cards right to stay alive, speaking ill of Victor Madigan isn't just dangerous—it's a death sentence for anyone who hears it and doesn't report it. With every word, Wolf draws us closer to the edge.

He's going to get us both killed.

Desperate to shift his thoughts, I lean in to distract him with my body once more, but he kisses me back fiercely, a wild light burning in his eyes. "No, I have a better idea for fun," he says, his grip tightening around me.

Dread pools in my stomach as he leads me from the room. I don't need to ask where we're headed; the destination is clear and filled with dark memories. We're going to see my mother, to the room that reeks of death despite the life-preserving fluids dripping into her veins.

"My enemies are still out of reach, but we can have fun with yours," Wolf snarls as we approach the door.

Only, it isn't fun. Not anymore, if it ever was. I still hate my mother, perhaps more than anyone else in the world. The bitterness toward my parents festers deep within me—they deserve every torment they encounter, or so I've told myself.

But seeing her like this, used as a pawn in Wolf's cruel games, stirs something unexpected in me—a flicker of conflict, a question of whether anyone truly deserves this kind of hell.

As I stand at the threshold of the room, the stench of despair and decay hits me like a physical blow. Inside, my mother is barely recognizable—her speech reduced to garbled cries and screams, her condition worsened by the constant torture Wolf inflicts using a cocktail of hallucinogens and stimulants. Her face, no longer pale but tinged yellow with jaundice, contorts unnaturally. Her movements are more akin to a wounded animal than a human.

As Wolf revels in his cruelty, I watch, detached, aware that any plea for mercy would only redirect his wrath toward me. Instead, I bide my time. He has consumed a lot of drugs today, and I wait until they claim him.

He leaves the cage, sweating, and slams the bolt on the door. His footsteps are awkward and sluggish, and when he turns to me, I smile and open my arms. He doesn't step into my open embrace; instead, he goes straight for the door. I know better than to linger, and I follow him to his bedroom.

It's a worse cage than the one my mother has found herself in.

He kicks off his shoes and lies down, throwing his arm over

his face. I watch until the rise and fall of his chest is even. I have often thought about killing him while he slept, but the sad truth is I know I wouldn't get away with it, even if I could do it.

The hall is silent as I make my way to my mother's cell— no friendly faces, no allies, just the echo of my footsteps. The smell grows stronger as I approach, a reminder of the inhumane conditions she's been kept in. When I reach the room, I head straight for the supply case filled with the drugs used to torment her.

I draw a vial—far more than any human could withstand. My hands are steady, my resolve firmer than it's ever been. But there is a child inside me who weeps and begs me to break.

I ignore her.

Standing before the cell, I meet my mother's frantic gaze. Her eyes, wide and darting, finally fix on the syringe in my hand. "You don't deserve this," I whisper, not sure if I'm trying to convince her or myself. "But I'm here to offer you a kindness you never offered me." The little girl wails, the one who experienced kindness from her. Memories that I must have suppressed charge back like an army protecting its land.

"The doll..." I whisper. My mother tilts her head; I don't know if she even understands me anymore.

"I loved that doll." I can picture it so clearly now—blonde pigtails, a white cap, and a blue and white dress. My stomach twists painfully. "You gave it to me." I blink tears, and the feel of the moisture on my cheeks startles me. I slept with that doll every night. What happened to it? I scour my memory, and it's like a movie that pauses. The doll is in my mother's hands; she's different now; my brother's death has changed everything. I cried as she released the doll into the lit fireplace. I watched a friend burn, a protector from the monsters, vanish before my eyes. I'm back to looking into my mother's tormented eyes. None of that matters now.

I hold up the syringe. "Let me end this for you." My bottom lip wobbles. I exhale a quick breath as time seems to slow as she processes my words, the implications. Then, with a resigned clarity in her tortured eyes, she extends her arm through the bars.

Relief, grief, and anger slam through me. She wants this to end. I have no parting words. No *I love you*, or *I'm sorry*. I don't love her, but what she has become is too much to bear.

As I administer the overdose, there's a silence between us that speaks louder than words ever could. Her grip on my hand is surprisingly gentle, a stark contrast to the harshness of our past. I stay with her, holding her gaze, as the life gradually fades from her eyes and her heart ceases its weary beating.

It's over. The room is silent, save for my own breathing. A part of me feels hollow, knowing the cycle of pain has finally ended, not with vengeance, but with an act of merciful release. As I stand there, the magnitude of what I've done—and what I still need to do—settles in. I know this isn't the end of my journey, but a grim chapter closed, paving the way for what must come next.

CHAPTER SEVENTEEN

Selene

The hours tick by—literally tick. Though the bedroom has a security door, the walls are too thin, and the sound of the grandfather clock in the corridor seeps into the room. The ticking claws at my skull as I bend over my laptop are relentless and unforgiving.

Tick tock. Tick tock.

It drives me mad. I glance at Niamh, who's dozing in the chair just under Sofia Hughes' photos, blissfully unaware of the chaos spiraling within me. I envy her peace; my own mind is an ever-tightening coil, wound by weeks of sleepless nights.

That damned medallion has taunted me for weeks. It murmurs

in my ear when I try to sleep, twisting my thoughts into dark knots of anxiety. Now that I have the key to unlock all its secrets, that infernal clock seems determined to hammer into my brain: "Too late, too long," it ticks, "you missed your chance."

No. I won't let it win. I slam my hands down on the desk, the smack echoing off the walls. Niamh jerks awake, startled, but I don't care.

"It's not too late," I mutter, my voice barely above a whisper. I'm the one who brought this to light. If it wasn't for me, that medallion would still be rotting away in some dusty drawer.

Niamh rubs her eyes and squints at me. "Selene, what's going on?"

The clock's relentless ticking is my heartbeat, drumming in my ears like a curse. I can't take it anymore. My hands tremble as I close my laptop and rise from my chair, walking purposefully to the bedroom door. I yank it open, and there it is, just steps away: the grandfather clock. Its pendulum sways with cruel precision.

Tick. Tock. Tick. Tock.

I step closer to the clock, pulling open its back panel. Cables and pulleys fill the space, tangled like nerves beneath the skin. I stare at them, vaguely aware they keep the mechanism going but unsure of how to silence it. I have no idea how this thing works so I do the only thing I can think of: I shove the clock with both hands.

The crash reverberates through the house. Glass shatters, wood splinters, and dull chimes that will never ring again echo in the chaos. I stand there, breathing heavily, staring at the remains of the clock.

Within moments, Niamh bursts through the bedroom door, her hand clutching her chest, eyes wide with panic. I hear footsteps racing up the stairs, and soon enough, the guards appear, confusion etched on their faces. I raise my hand and shout, "Stop!"

They hesitate, but I fix them with a glare that brooks no argument. "I don't need you. I need peace."

Without waiting for a response, I brush past Niamh and stride back to my chair, collapsing into it with a sigh. I close my eyes and lean my head back, savoring the newfound silence. Finally. Blessed silence.

"Selene, are you all right?" Niamh's voice quivers with concern, but I don't open my eyes.

"Shh," I hush her. "Do you hear that?"

It's silence I hear, like I expected.

Niamh's confusion is almost palpable. "No...?"

"Me, either. It's perfect." My voice is steady, almost serene, but the look on Niamh's face makes it clear I'm scaring her. Her brow creases with worry, her lips pressing into a thin line. She's been so patient, keeping the tea and coffee flowing as I scroll through document after document. Her unspoken concern is obvious, but I remain glued to my laptop.

Ever since we returned from the museum earlier this morning, I've been trying to unravel why John Dee's language—the supposed language of the angels—is inscribed on the medallion. Page upon page, my eyes burning, fingers aching, I've combed through everything I could find.

Dinner passed in a blur, with Niamh practically forcing a roast beef sandwich and celery into my hands. But I hardly noticed the food as I devoured the words on the screen instead.

Diarmuid hasn't come home. Probably just as well, considering the wreckage of the clock still sprawled across the hallway.

Eventually, Niamh gives up on keeping me company and goes to bed, leaving me alone with my thoughts and the rustling of pages.

It's an hour from dawn when the sound of footsteps reaches my ears. My eyes snap open, my senses immediately on edge.

"I said I didn't need you!" I yell into the dark, spinning around to face the door. My pulse races, adrenaline surging through my veins. The clock is long gone, so what is causing that noise?

Without looking up from my laptop, I bark again, "I said I didn't need you!" But when I don't hear anyone retreating, I spring up from my desk, prepared to slam the door shut. I freeze, though, when I see Diarmuid's dark eyes watching me intently from the doorway.

"Oh! It's you!" I exclaim, excitement bursting in my chest as I practically bounce in place. "Okay, so I've translated the text. It says, 'Luíonn an dorn ag Sí an Bhrú.' I think. Enochian doesn't have any accents or diacritics, so it took a while to piece together. But I did figure out that it's supposed to be Irish."

His gaze shifts to the broken clock in the hallway, and he frowns. "Why is this door open?"

Ignoring his question, I plow on, unable to contain my enthusiasm. "I don't speak Irish, though my grandfather would be thrilled if I did. But I recognize it, so that helped. The phrase means, 'The fist rests at Sí an Bhrú.'"

Diarmuid's brow furrows as he steps forward. "There's a lock on this door for a reason, Selene."

But I'm too excited to notice his tone. I reach for a stack of papers beside the printer and shove them into his hands. "Now, Sí an Bhrú is the old Irish name for Newgrange, which is incredibly convenient because it's just a quick zip up the M2 from here. Less than an hour, I think!"

He skims the pages quickly, his brow creasing even deeper. "You're not listening."

"I am. I am. Just let me finish telling you this." My words tumble out in a rush as I push back my exhaustion, the thrill of discovery filling me with a manic energy. "Newgrange's old name, Sí an Bhrú, means 'Womb of the Boyne,' after the river near the site. This is where I'm struggling—how far do I translate? Do I stop at Newgrange or should I investigate what happened along the river?"

I pace in front of Diarmuid, my excitement bubbling over as my mind races through the possibilities. "And then it hit me."

His brow lifts, but I don't give him time to interject. I'm practically bouncing on my toes, my voice breathless and hurried. "Newgrange is said to be the burial mound for Dagda Mór of the Tuatha Dé Danann and his three sons. The Tuatha Dé Danann, Diarmuid! The ancient rulers of Ireland! They were powerful, magical. If the Hands of Kings has existed since the dawn of human history, then maybe there's something at Newgrange!"

Diarmuid opens his mouth to speak, but I cut him off with

a hasty, "Shh!" I can't afford to lose momentum now. He needs to understand.

"I know you're probably going to reprimand me for something or other," I continue, my eyes fixed on his, "but just listen. The Tuatha Dé Danann could be the key. If the Hands of Kings truly has roots stretching back to their time, Newgrange might hold more than just ancient tombs. There could be answers, Diarmuid!"

"This theory seemed absolutely crazy until I found copies of Dr. Michael O'Kelley's original notes," I say, pulling a page from my pile and handing it to Diarmuid.

He takes the page and scans it silently, his brows knitting together as he reads.

"Dr. O'Kelley notes here and here," I point out, jabbing my finger at the faded handwriting, "that he suspected a tunnel to an even older structure than Newgrange. Newgrange was built around 3200 BC, Diarmuid. There might be a tunnel near the entrance that leads to something older."

I pause to gauge his reaction, but he's still focused on the document.

"But what does that have to do with today? With now?" I press, pulling out another page and offering it to him.

Diarmuid looks at me questioningly before taking the second document. His eyes quickly scan the page, and I can see the tension rising in his posture.

"Edict VI of the Hands of Kings states," I continue, "'Kings are made to lead our world, but they must be guided. One Hand shall place the Kings in their places. One Hand shall make Kings.

One Hand shall destroy Kings.' One Hand should make. One Hand should destroy. The medallion mentions the Fist."

I can hardly contain my excitement as I explain. "I think Rian was right; there's a council above Victor. 'The Fist rests at Sí an Bhrú.' Victor is the Hand, and this council is the Fist."

Diarmuid's gaze snaps up to mine, his eyes wide.

"Victor's father was the Hand, and so was his father before him, on and on," I continue. "If the Fist rests at Newgrange, I'd bet everything that they're burying the council members there. If we can find even one name, we can trace their descendants to current family members and uncover the council. We can go above Victor's head. We could find a way to take control."

I feel like panting after spilling everything out so quickly. It all makes sense, and I'm so proud of myself. Weeks of being stumped, and finally, one clue unlocked the whole puzzle. I've done it. I've cracked it.

Diarmuid places the pages I gave him carefully on top of my desk, but his expression is grave.

"I told you to keep this door locked," he says quietly.

My head snaps up, disbelief flaring inside me. The triumph I felt moments ago vanishes. "Are you fucking serious?" I yell, my voice echoing off the walls as the papers in my arms scatter in all directions.

His face hardens. "Yes, I'm serious. Selene, you're so focused on unraveling this conspiracy that you're forgetting the risks. The door was open. Victor could have sent anyone in here, and you'd be none the wiser until it was too late." He marches away and locks the door before returning to me.

"And you think that's more important than what I just showed you?" I pace in a tight circle, seething with frustration. "I'm onto something huge, Diarmuid! We have a real chance of uncovering the council. Why can't you see that?"

"I do see that, but none of it will matter if you're dead." He steps closer, his fists clenched at his sides. "This isn't some academic exercise where we can afford to be careless. You and Niamh are doing everything possible to get yourselves killed."

I bristle, my nails digging into my palms. "Do you really think I'm being reckless? You're not taking my work seriously! I've pieced together clues that could bring down Victor's entire operation, and all you care about is whether the door is locked."

"Because the threat is real!" His voice rises, and he's inches away now, towering over me. "Victor is dangerous, Selene. He's made that clear, and he's willing to go after anyone to protect his power. You're not just putting yourself at risk; you're putting Niamh at risk, too."

"Niamh knows the risks," I snap back. "She's chosen to help me, and we're both willing to do whatever it takes to see this through."

"That's the problem," Diarmuid says through gritted teeth. "You're willing to gamble with your lives as if this were some game. But it's not a game, Selene. Victor already threatened you once, and he'll follow through on those threats if we're not careful."

The room feels too small, and I can hear Niamh's faint

knocking at the door. "Selene? Diarmuid? Is everything all right?" she calls out, but I can't answer her right now.

"You're letting fear cloud your judgment," I spit out. "We can't waste time hiding behind locked doors. If we don't act quickly, we could lose our chance to find the council."

"Fear keeps us alive!" he snaps. "I'm not saying we shouldn't investigate Newgrange, but we can't afford to rush headlong into danger without a plan."

"And who's going to make that plan, Diarmuid?" I scoff. "You? You're so terrified of taking a risk that you'd have us sit around doing nothing!"

"I'm trying to protect you," he says, his voice thick with emotion. "Can't you see that?"

"I don't need your protection!" I shout, tears welling up despite my resolve. "I need you to believe in me."

He's silent for a moment, breathing heavily as he struggles to rein in his anger. "I do believe in you," he says finally. "But I can't just stand by and watch you charge into danger without a care for your own safety."

"Then maybe you should just stand back," I say bitterly. "I'm going to Newgrange, with or without your help."

The room falls silent, and for a moment, we both stare at each other, breathless and furious. The door rattles as Niamh tries the handle again.

Diarmuid's eyes burn with frustration. "This entire situation is more complicated than your little quest," he says, his voice low and controlled. "There is a lot in play here, and you aren't even part of the game."

Condescension drips from his words, and it's like a slap across my face. "Excellent approach! Condescension! I love it," I retort, my sarcasm razor-sharp. "Would you like me to skip off to the kitchen, my lord? Stay in my place?"

His gaze darkens, and before I can blink, his hands are on either side of my face, pushing me back against the wall, his body pressed close to mine. His breath is hot against my skin as he leans in, his eyes locked on mine.

"I want you to give the most minimum fuck about your life," he growls. "You may not give a shit about what happens to you, but I do. If you can't live for yourself, live for me!"

His voice vibrates with intensity, and my breath catches in my throat. I stare into his eyes, my pulse quickening as his words sink in. The anger in his voice is matched only by the fear and longing flickering beneath the surface.

A shiver runs down my spine, and I whisper, "I do want to live for you, Diarmuid. But this matters to me. All of it. And you agreed to help me."

His grip softens, his forehead resting against mine as he breathes heavily. "I did," he says quietly. He's silent for a long moment, and I can feel the tension trembling between us like a live wire.

Finally, he tilts his head up, and his lips find mine. The kiss is fierce and raw, and I melt into him, my anger dissolving into a desperate yearning. His fingers thread through my hair, pulling me closer as my hands curl around his shoulders, holding on tight.

After a breathless eternity, he breaks the kiss and murmurs against my lips, "Give me a week. I'll get us where we need to be at Newgrange."

I nod, my fingers tracing the curve of his jaw. "One week."

CHAPTER EIGHTEEN

Niamh

The door to the research room never opened for me. Diarmuid and Selene's shouting match had died down, but they still hadn't left. My stomach tightens as the silence stretches on, and I know that means they settled everything. They probably ended up even closer.

Which means, I failed.

I clutch the broom tighter, fighting back tears as I start sweeping up the broken glass in the hallway. One shard glints in the dim light, jagged and cruel, like a dagger into my heart. After I clear the last splintered piece, I turn to the grandfather clock lying on its side. Its wooden frame is damaged, and the once-proud clock now stands lopsided, its cables and pulleys hopelessly tangled. Not a tick, not a sound. Just a silent, mocking reminder that time had run out. My time.

I had noticed it for the first time in Selene's apartment the way they gravitated towards each other. I've never felt like a third wheel with them, but that night. I really had. It wasn't just his touch; it was how they started like they were the only two people in the world or how he kissed her differently than me.

With shaking hands, I gather the shattered glass and dump it in the bathroom trash can, leaving the broom and dustpan in the hallway. My head feels like it's stuffed with cotton. Mechanically, I shuffle into the master bedroom and collapse onto the bed. My arm reaches out on instinct, fingers brushing the pillow where Diarmuid's head used to rest.

My chest heaves, and the tears start to fall, leaving a damp stain on the pillowcase. Hot, salty rivers that I can't hold back anymore.

Ella could be next, I think through the sobs. If I don't find a way to be useful to the Hand of Kings, they could take her instead. The image of my sister being handed over, her fear, her confusion of why I didn't stop it is enough to send my heart skyrocketing.

The thought is a bitter one, sinking deep into the pit of my stomach. My failure means I couldn't secure her future, and it feels like I've let her down in the worst way possible. The whole situation is so unfair.

I curl up tighter, trying to contain my grief as the tears come again, flooding through me with a force that leaves me shaking.

What a tired and tragic world this is, this world of women. We like to convince ourselves that we're in charge of our destinies, but our fates are bound up in everyone else's choices. I've been trained to be competitive, but not like this. No, I was thrown into an arena for a sport I never learned to play.

And all the while, my parents sit back and reap the rewards of the hell I'm going through. I didn't sign up for this. In my wildest dreams, I could never have imagined being handed a sentence so messed up. The deeper we dig into Diarmuid's world, the more I want to run, but I have no where to run to. I have no one to turn to. I have no one…. I have Ella, and she is worth protecting.

A bitter taste rises in my throat as I sit up and wipe away my tears. I can't control what the cult decides, but I can confront two people who are responsible for all of this.

I quickly get dressed and head downstairs, each step growing firmer with purpose. The murmur of voices in the lobby reaches my ears before I see them—a few guards playing cards. They jump up, startled, as soon as I step into view.

"I want to see my parents," I say, my voice steady and unwavering, a complete contradiction to the tide of anger and pain that rides hard and fast inside me.

One of the guards looks confused and shifts his gaze to the others as if seeking the other guards' approval first before he makes his decision. After a pause, and a conversation that only seems to take place with looks and nods, I'm motioned by another guard.

"Let's go," the guard says gruffly, gesturing for me to follow.

I square my shoulders, keeping my eyes fixed ahead. The resolve hardens within me as I imagine the confrontation. It's time my parents understood the cost of their ambitions, the scars etched deeply into my skin. I can't allow Ella's youthful skin to be marred with their greed.

The streets are empty as I'm driven toward the house where I was raised. The headlights cast a dim glow on the vacant pavement, and my protectors sit silently beside me in the car. It's the middle of the night, and the guards didn't even question this sudden journey—they've learned over the past few weeks that Selene and I both tend to go places impulsively. But unlike them, I'm questioning my decision more than ever. Returning home feels like pulling at a knot that could either unravel smoothly or tighten around my neck.

We pull into the driveway, and as I step out into the night air, a chill grips me, and my breath forms a cloud in front of my face. The smell of the sea fills my lungs and brings me strength. After all, I was made for the water, and I miss the smell of it so much. I glance back in the direction where I know the water rages against the rock side. I can't see it, but I can picture the slashing of waves, making their mark in the landscape, like some form of script that only Mother Nature can decipher.

Motion sensor lights flick on, illuminating the Tudor-style woodwork at the peak of the facade. The sudden lighting brings me back to the reason I am here. My mind wanders to my real reason. Is it the understanding that Diarmuid won't pick me that fuels my anger, or the thought of Ella going to the highest bidder? I ring the doorbell repeatedly, aggressively. Both. It's both, I realize.

I hear one of the guards starting to open the car door, but I snap, "Stay in the car and keep it running!"

The door swings open, and my father stands there, tightening his robe around his body, his face etched with confusion. My mother hurries down the hallway behind him, her expression just as bewildered.

"Niamh? What the hell are you—" my father begins as he rubs the sleep out of his eyes.

"No," I cut him off. "I'm talking. You are listening. Ella is not a bargaining chip."

"What?" my mother stammers, her voice tinged with disbelief. "Niamh, what are you—"

"I'm still talking!" I snarl. My anger feels like fire in my veins, and I let it burn. "Whatever deal you made for me, you won't make it for Ella. She will live a normal life and have all the opportunities that you denied me. All of them. Any of them. If she wants to keep doing ballet, she'll keep doing ballet. If she wants to be a bloody clown, she will be a clown."

My father squares his shoulders and glares down at me, his voice cold and commanding. "That is not for you to decide."

"NOR IS IT FOR YOU!" I shout, my voice echoing down the empty street. "I am not the same timid girl who left this house. You will let her live her life. And if you need another Bride to give them, give yourselves. No one will touch Ella."

I glare at my mother. How would she feel if she was handed over to some man to do with what he wishes?

My father's face contorts with anger. "You ungrateful—"

"Trust me, I am grateful. So fucking grateful. I'm grateful for the lessons you taught me. Never quit. Always go for the gold. Endure the pain. All of this has come in handy over the last few months. And you also taught me how to be a good parent. I will do the exact opposite of everything you did."

His eyes narrow, and his jaw clenches. "I'm calling the police."

I step closer, a smirk curling at the corner of my mouth. "What will you tell them, Father? That the daughter you sold to a cult has come to her own home to tell you how fucked up you are?" I let that sink in before I continue, my voice a low, threatening growl. "You are lucky I'm here because this is your warning. I will be watching you, and you better not fuck up Ella like you fucked up me."

I don't give him a chance to respond. I yank the door shut, cutting off his sputtering retort. I hear the door reopen behind me, but I don't turn back as he shouts into the night, spewing his fury like poison. Instead, I walk calmly toward the car, my head high and my heart racing. The guards watch me, wide-eyed, as I slide into the back seat and slam the door shut.

"Drive," I command, and the engine roars to life, leaving behind the shouts of a desperate man in the distance. I catch a glimpse of my father's enraged silhouette shrinking in the rearview mirror.

Will my words sink in? I have no idea, but I need to remember they are afraid of the cult, and I can use that to my advantage to keep Ella safe. I can pretend I have some sway if another conversation presents itself.

The engine hums softly as we cruise down the empty streets, the headlights cutting a path through the darkness. The tension from my confrontation still lingers, but it's mingled with a sense of triumph. I stare out the window at the passing city, my pulse slowly steadying.

I've never stood up to my parents in my life. I've never stood up to anyone and that is a flaw I am determined to correct. No more nice Niamh.

I catch the driver's gaze in the rearview mirror. He's smiling, the corners of his mouth curling with amusement.

"I have a brother you can yell at if you're still feeling spunky," he quips, the smile reaching his eyes.

I can't help but laugh, shaking my head as I sink back into the seat. "Bring me every mother, father, brother, sister, and fucked-up cousin. I'll take them all on."

His chuckle joins mine, a shared moment of lightness in the dark night. The road stretches ahead, but I have an unshakeable certainty that whatever lies beyond, I'll be ready.

CHAPTER NINETEEN

Diarmuid

The bed in this guest room was clearly designed for two, but I've grown spoiled by the custom mattress in my master suite. Still, I don't mind sharing space when it's Selene I'm pressed so closely to. Her lavender-scented hair is the first thing I breathe in as I wake, and the fragrance wraps around me, comforting yet stirring something deep inside. I linger for a moment, watching the soft rise and fall of her chest, savoring the warmth of her skin.

I'm a King, and a King is supposed to have a chosen Consort, a woman who would share his secrets and help continue the family line. Every day, it feels more and more like it should be Selene.

I run my hand through her hair, and she sighs in her sleep. Selene is impossible, reckless. She takes unfathomable risks to get what she wants. How dangerous would it be to choose a woman exactly like me?

I slip out of bed quietly and head to my own room. The absence of Niamh catches me by surprise. She's usually there, vigilant and punctual. I shake my head and head to the shower. Warm water cascades down my body, clearing away the tension. By the time I'm dressed and heading downstairs, I've already planned my day.

In the living room, I find Niamh sprawled on one of the couches, an empty carton of ice cream abandoned on the coffee table. The Netflix screensaver gently illuminates her sleeping form. I frown and make a mental note to address this later.

From the corner of my eye, one of my men approaches.

"You have a guest waiting for you in the foyer."

It's too early for visitors, and I feel my irritation mounting as I adjust my sleeves and head out.

The sight of Father Isaac Waryn, standing there serenely with his arms clasped behind his back, ignites my fury. This is a man who should have never contacted me again, let alone shown up at my home unannounced.

"Clear the foyer," I order my guards, my voice cold and firm. They hesitate briefly before scattering, leaving me alone with the man who once betrayed me.

"Father," I say, the word dripping with disdain, "what business do you think you have here?"

Isaac seems to sense my fury and raises his hands defensively, his eyes darting from me to the empty foyer behind him. His voice is measured but trembling. "I know I shouldn't be here."

My eyes narrow as I take a step closer, and my words are like venom, sharp and cutting. "Lesser men than you have disappeared for disobeying me."

Isaac swallows hard, then straightens himself. "Someone came to my church looking for Brien Cahill."

He pauses, letting the name hang in the air like a lingering echo. The anger in my chest tightens into a knot—Brien Cahill—a boy that Victor ordered killed. I took the job because that's what I'm trained to do. But killing children is something I've never been okay with.

Instead, I helped Isaac and Brien's parents smuggle the boy out of the country, finding sanctuary with distant relatives in the States. In doing so, I directly disobeyed Victor's orders, an act of rebellion that could have cost me everything. But I was tired of seeing children pay for the sins of their fathers.

Kane Cahill, Brien's father, owed the Kings a significant amount in gambling debt, and after a year without paying up, Victor ordered a hit on the man's son. I couldn't stomach it, couldn't watch another innocent life be destroyed.

I square my shoulders and focus my gaze on Isaac. "What did you tell the man who visited you?"

Isaac's face is a mask of worry. "I told him I presided over Brien's funeral and could confirm that he is dead."

His voice lowers as he glances at the floor. "But I don't think he believes me, Mr. O'Sullivan. I sincerely believe that the man knows Brien Cahill is still alive."

The weight of his words settles over me like a suffocating fog. If they suspect Brien is still out there, they'll come for him again. And if they find out I've deceived Victor, I'm as good as dead.

"Who was this man?" I ask. The one who delivered the news.

The priest rattles off a description that could be a million normal men.

My rage is quiet, a swirling whirlpool awaiting an unfortunate soul's fall from a vessel. Isaac shifts nervously, sensing the tension simmering beneath the surface.

"What will you do?" he asks, his voice barely a whisper.

"Thank you for your information, Father. Your service will not be forgotten." The words are sharp and final, and I dismiss him with a wave.

The priest hesitates. His duty to the cloth and his duty as a man evidently seem to be battling under his skin. But I don't have time to console him or guarantee him that Brien will be safe. That is a promise I can't make.

His shoulders sag forward in defeat, and he gives one final nod of his head before walking across the foyer, I watch until the front door closes and one of my men enters the foyer.

"Get me a car," I say without turning to him.

The Cahills' residence is my destination. It's a small stone house with plastic flowers in the soil and statues of animals scattered among the bushes. The facade is as fake as the father who resides there.

The car rolls up beside the cur,b and before it comes to a full stop, I open the back door and step out onto the sidewalk. The small gate that guards their home has gray peeled paint flaked along the ground. I step over it, not wanting any of the paint to stick to my black shoes. The canopy above my head over the front door shelters me from the sun, and I raise my hand and knock three times on the stained yellow glass. I see the shimmer of an outline move closer and take a step back.

Mrs. Cahill answers the door, and her face drains of color as recognition flickers in her eyes. She remembers. How could she forget? Last time we saw each other, I was sent to kill her son—and I laid out her husband in the middle of a church.

"Is Kane home?" I ask, my voice steady and low.

She shakes her head frantically. "No, he isn't."

I don't say anything else. Instead, I turn to leave, but she follows, clutching at my arm. "Please, what has happened?" she begs.

Her grip tightens around my sleeve, and I turn to her with eyes blazing in fury.

The look alone makes her collapse in the yard, covering her face and drowning in tears. I don't linger to comfort her; there's no solace in this for any of us. Whether she thinks something happened to her son, or knows what will happen to her husband, it takes her to her knees. I don't confirm or deny anything. I make my way to the car, and we pull away from the house.

Kane Cahill is a man controlled by his addiction, a slave to a vice that drags him away from his duties as a husband and father. There are a few places in Dublin where someone like Kane can find solace, where the prying eyes of the world can't reach.

But the Kings see all.

It takes a few tries, reaching out to contacts to find out where he is. I finally get an answer.

He's hiding in the backroom of a laundromat, and that's where my driver takes me.

The smell of stale smoke and sweat hangs heavy in the air, and the murmur of conversation dies as soon as I enter.

"Everybody out." The command slips from my lips, and the room clears within seconds. No one fights me on it. No one stays to defend Kane Cahill.

Kane remains seated at the table, his eyes glazed and his hands absentmindedly turning over the cards in front of him. He doesn't seem to notice that his companions have abandoned him or that the room has fallen silent. I step closer, my shadow casting long over the table. He's so consumed with his cards and greed that he is none the wiser.

"Kane," I say quietly, my voice cutting through the fog of his stupor.

His head jerks up, and for a moment, confusion flashes across his face before recognition sets in. He swallows, eyes darting around the room, and then he meets my gaze.

"Diarmuid," he stammers, "what brings you here?"

But the guilt in his voice betrays the lie behind his words. He knows exactly why I'm here.

He has told someone that his son is alive and he escaped the clutches of the Hands of Kings.

That can't happen.

The room falls silent, and Kane's gaze flickers nervously as I advance toward him. Without hesitation, I knock the table across the room, sending cards and empty bottles scattering against the walls. Kane flinches and recoils, scrambling to his feet as the whirlpool swallows the vessel completely.

"You haven't learned," I growl, my voice low and seething with barely contained rage. "Your son was spared by my mercy. I risked my own life to save Brien, and here you are, back to your old ways."

He tries to speak, his words slurred and disjointed, but I cut him off sharply. "The debt must be paid, and Brien will not be the one paying it."

His eyes widen as the gravity of my words sinks in. I grip him by the collar and drag him across the room. He doesn't have the strength to resist, his pleas barely audible over the thundering of my pulse. I spin him fully, his back pressing into my chest.

He tries to speak, but there isn't one word that would make me stop. With one fluid movement, I slip the blade from the hidden compartment in my trousers pocket, and with a rage that gives me strength, I plunge it cleanly into his neck. He gurgles, blood making a pathway out of his mouth. His hands try to pry mine off him, but his attempt is weak as the life and blood seep out of him. I release him, and he hits the ground hard.

I fall to my knees as blood spews up out of his mouth. His

hands try to stop the flow of blood from his neck. Easily, I pull his hands away and use the knife as a saw, cutting through flesh, veins, and tissue all the way to his bones. I use my foot to break his neck.

The ordeal is gruesome and bloody. It didn't have to end this way, but in order to save Brien, Kane left me no choice.

Not long afterward, I walk through St. Gertrude's church, my coat bundled tightly in my arms. I pass the cleaners standing along the aisle, their eyes following me with a mixture of suspicion and fear. Each one is armed and ready to defend Victor with their lives. Their gazes trail to the blood that I can't hide on the sleeves of my shirt or the small spots that managed to land on the front of my chest.

The stone walls are cool to the touch as I walk past the altar, down the hallway, through the private courtyard, and into Victor's office.

Victor is seated at his desk, writing on some document, as two of his guards stand vigil at the door. He looks up as I enter, his eyes narrowing with suspicion. Without breaking stride, I boldly walk the length of the office, step up to the desk, and unfurl my coat.

Kane's head tumbles out, landing with a sickening thud on top of Victor's papers. Blood smears across the document, and the guards gasp in shock. But I don't flinch.

"The debt has been paid," I declare, my voice firm and unyielding. "Brien Cahill is not to be touched."

Victor says nothing but quietly lays his pen down. As the

fire blazes within me, he returns my gaze with an emotionless coldness, the same gaze that watched me as he held my hands over the candle so many times, knowing how my skin would tighten and twist from the hot flame. Knowing the pain he inflicted on a child but unwilling to stop it.

A beat passes in silence. The room feels like it's holding its breath. Then, without another word, I turn and leave. The guards remain frozen, and no one dares to stop me.

Outside, the air is sharp with the chill of morning, and I walk away from the church, knowing that Victor will have to think carefully before deciding his next move. The whirlpool has claimed its victim, but I remain firmly in control of the tide.

CHAPTER TWENTY

Amira

I expected this kind of thing to happen at night. The darkness makes a good shroud for evil, doesn't it? But here I am, walking onto this ferry in broad daylight.

I pull my scarf tighter around my neck against the wind. It's cold enough to slice through my thin sweater, but I welcome it. The air dulls the searing pain from the beating Wolf gave me when he found out I'd destroyed his favorite toy. My clothing sticks to the wounds like glue, and each step on the metal deck is a small agony. The drugs numb the rest. I've taken just enough to blur the world into a hazy dream, where even the worst horrors float by like mist.

Wolf explained that we were doing this during the day because the docks are bustling now. The noise, the crowds, the constant activity—it all makes for the perfect camouflage. I try not to think about what's coming, what I will be a part of.

The ferry looks like any other ferry, the kind that shuttles tourists between Dublin, Wales, Liverpool, and the Isle of Man. But when we slip below deck, I realize how different this one really is. Women are huddled around the walls, half-standing, half-sitting, their hands tied to a wooden rail. Some look healthy, others emaciated. All of them are terrified. Their eyes dart to us, and they recoil, trying to press themselves back against the wall as if they could disappear through it.

One of them looks at me, and I see surprise flicker in her eyes. I can just imagine they don't see many women when they are being trafficked. I don't want to see hope there, hope that I can save her because I fucking can't. I can't even save myself from this fate. I glance away, but I'm faced with more faces; my stomach curls, and I focus on Wolf.

He talks to a couple of men, and I know they're the ones in charge, as they were in this room when we entered. Each man carries himself like he's a god. After a brief conversation that I can't hear over my heart pounding in my ears, Wolf finally makes his way over to me, and before I can react, he kisses me deeply. It's not a kiss that speaks of love or tenderness. It's feral, almost animalistic. It's a statement of possession, his claim on me, and it goes on far too long. I fight the urge to gag, but I hold my breath and let him devour me until he finally pulls away, taking my hand to lead me around the room.

His grip is firm, possessive. "Do you see any that catch your eye?" he asks, gesturing at the women.

My pulse quickens as I scan their faces. Their eyes search mine for any hint of mercy. "My eye?" I ask as if I don't understand.

I flinch when Wolf murmurs in my ear, "Yes, my sweet, you are choosing today." My stomach knots painfully. This is a new form of torture—forcing me to choose which souls will be dragged into the same hell I live in. It's bad enough being his, a plaything, a punching bag. I've seen the abuse the others endure at the brothel. I've had to distract him from hurting the ones who look like me. But now, staring into their frightened faces, I must decide who will join me in this nightmare.

My hesitation is all he needs to feed on my discomfort. I catch the twisted smile curling across his lips before he points to a girl across the room. "I want her," he announces. But that's no woman. Her face is too round, her body too slender. She starts speaking quickly in a language I don't recognize, tears welling in her wide eyes.

Wolf steps toward her. A panic grips me. I glance at the other men in the room, their greedy eyes sizing up the "cargo" instead of seeing the people in front of them. As monstrous as Wolf is, at least I can redirect him when he turns violent. If these women fall into the other men's hands, there will be no one to protect them. I wish I could walk away or clamp down on the panic that tears through me, but I'm here in this room with the knowledge of what will happen to these woman.

My voice cracks as I announce, "I want them all." I step

forward, my gaze fixed on Wolf, trying to appear confident. I won't let them become victims if I can help it.

A chorus of yelling erupts from the men, a mix of English and other languages. They're gesturing furiously, insisting that this isn't the deal. Wolf can't have them all. My pulse races, and I step up to one of them, a man whose eyes burn with anger. I know I need to make my mark; I need to show my authority. Without thinking, I raise my hand and slap him across the face. The sound bounces off the metal walls. All the earlier tears from the woman cease, and the only sound for a second is their audible gasps of shock. I think I'm more shocked myself that I didn't notice the man clear the small distance between us.

He grabs my arm and twists it painfully, making me cry out. But Wolf is on him in an instant, his fist smashing into the man's jaw. Each thump makes me grin. I rub my arm as I watch Wolf throw all his weight against every single punch.

The other man jumps into action. That I hadn't expected. With only their words, they try to defend their comrade, but they quickly come to their senses when Wolf releases the man he was beating, and his body hits the floor with a heavy thud. Wolf looks at each of them with heavy breaths. He reminds me of a fire-breathing dragon. I shiver internally. I have witnessed what happens when you piss him off. Despite his recent demotion, Wolf still belongs to the Kings, and no one dares to cross them.

To drive his position home, he grabs another man who had spoken the loudest.

I clutch my throbbing arm, watching as Wolf beats the second man into submission, his fists raining down like hammer blows. I should feel relief, knowing that he's protecting me, but instead, I'm sickened. How long can I keep up this charade, pretending I have any control? How much longer can I bear this reality? How much longer can I stand by and watch so much wrath unleashed on innocent women?

Wolf finally stops and releases the second man, who doesn't fall to the floor. He clutches his broken nose and races from the room. Humiliation and, I'm sure shock, turning his face red. Wolf glances around the room, and his gaze lands on me, his expression still wild. He stands straighter and fixes his suit jacket before walking to me. He grabs my chin roughly, forcing me to meet his gaze. "You see, my sweet? You needn't worry. I'll always take care of you."

His words are a mockery, a twisted reminder of my captivity. But I swallow my fear and nod obediently. He can't know what's stirring inside me.

I cross my arms, forcing a sense of calm into my posture as I approach one girl. She's on the floor, her wrists tied above her head. Tears stream down her cheeks, but I keep my face a mask of indifference. I flex my foot so that the tip of my shoe tilts her chin up.

"This one is mine," I declare, letting my voice drip with the kind of cold, possessive cruelty I've learned from Wolf. "My new toy."

Wolf barks a laugh behind me, his heavy footsteps echoing on the metal floor as he comes up and wraps his arm around my waist. His lips press against my neck, and I shudder as his erection through his jeans against my backside. "Yes. Claim her," he growls into my ear, his breath hot against my skin.

The man he had beaten groans on the ground not too far away, but I can't look away from the girl I have just claimed.

Her eyes, wide with fear, stare up at me, and I meet her gaze with a look of icy detachment. I have to play my role perfectly. Right now, I am Wolf's companion, his equal in cruelty. But beneath the surface, I'm forming a plan.

I glance at Wolf, letting my lips curl into a smile as if relishing the power over the terrified girl before me. But inside, the walls of my mind are already shifting and rearranging. If I can convince him of my loyalty, if I can make him believe that I'm on his side, maybe I can gain enough control to unlock the chains that bind us all.

We're all in cages, but somewhere, there's a key, and I'm determined to find it. To hold it. And when the moment is right, I will open every door and burn this nightmare to the ground. I'll play this part as long as it takes. Wolf's kiss feels like a branding iron against my neck, and his grip tightens as he presses himself closer.

"You always have the best taste," he murmurs, his words a snake's hiss.

I laugh softly, a sound as cold and hollow as I can make it. "Only the best," I reply, my voice steady.

CHAPTER TWENTY-ONE

The universe winks at me. Here I am, at Newgrange, a place as ancient as time itself, feeling every bit the intruder in a land of historical whispers. The walk from where we parked, discreetly away from the main site, taxes me more than I'd like to admit. Niamh and Diarmuid, however, seem unfazed by the distance or the chill that clings to the Irish air like a persistent fog.

Keeping pace with them is a matter of pride. Diarmuid, particularly, moves with an effortless grace, a silent sentinel. Despite the load he carries—a pack laden with shovels, picks, and various other tools necessary for our undisclosed activities— he makes no noise. He's wrapped each item in untreated leather, ensuring no metal clinks against another, a testament to his meticulous nature.

Beside me, Niamh strides with a newfound confidence that radiates off her like the dawn. Her chin is up, her eyes bright with secrets and possibilities. Just a few days ago, something changed in her, a subtle shift that brought a bounce to her step and a constant, mysterious smile to her lips.

Curiosity gets the better of me. "Did something happen?" I ask.

Diarmuid glances at us but resumes his silent walk. I know he is listening, and I should wait until Niamh and I are alone, but her energy is like a tug on mine, and I need to know what has changed.

Her response is a cryptic smile as she squeezes my hand. "I'm not one hundred percent sure how it will work out yet, but I'll keep you updated."

Now, our hands are linked again, our arms swinging in unison as we navigate the path. The connection feels grounding, a silent affirmation of our shared journey. I don't press further. The landscape around us is a mix of shadow and soft light, the ancient stones of Newgrange casting long, solemn shadows that feel like they stretch back through millennia.

The early December day had been unusually warm, a brief respite that felt almost like a tease when the night brought with it a sharp, biting cold front. Temperatures plummeted, transforming the day's leftover dew into a crisp layer of frost that crunches underfoot as we make our way through the field. The stark chill seeps through my boots, numbing my toes.

Above, the stars blaze with an intensity that illuminates the landscape in a celestial glow, allowing me to just discern the lazy meander of the River Boyne beside us. Ahead, the ancient silhouette of Newgrange rises, a stark outline against the dark sky. We approach from the back, the front hidden from view, but a mysterious glow hints at activity on the other side of the tomb, its source unseen but deeply felt.

The air here is charged, almost electric, as if the very night itself whispers secrets of ages past. The countless stars, eternal witnesses, seem to watch us with silent, knowing glances, their twinkling almost conspiratorial.

As we reach the circle of large stones that encircle the site, the supernatural feeling intensifies. Each monolith is carved with symbols—spirals that seem to dance in the moonlight, diamonds that catch the frost, turning them into glistening jewels in the night. The frost adds a delicate sheen, making the carvings stand out starkly against the rough texture of the stones. I can't resist; I extend my hand, tracing the cold, intricate swirls, feeling the pulse of history under my fingertips.

These symbols, debated endlessly by historians, speak of an ancient wisdom, perhaps a purpose long forgotten. What did this place mean to those who built it? A temple? A tomb? A calendar? The stones hold their secrets tightly.

As we circle to the front, guided by Diarmuid's confident step and Niamh's quiet awe, the outer facade of Newgrange comes into view, bathed in the otherworldly glow from the other side. The photo in my file doesn't do justice to the imposing beauty of these age-old stones under the cloak of night. The tomb's grandeur is humbling, its presence a heavy weight in the silent night.

Lorcan's words at the Harvest Moon ceremony echo in my mind. *The Hand of Kings has been in existence since Mesopotamia.* A civilization dating back to 10,000 BC, where no written evidence could have survived to tell us of their secret societies, their covert practices. Yet here I am, touching a relic just as enigmatic, just as ancient, wondering if those reaching out from the past had grasped the same truths we seek today.

What did they know? What whispers lay hidden in the stone and frost? These questions swirl through my mind as my fingers glide over the cold patterns, each one a potential key to unlocking the enigmas of the past.

As I trace my fingers along the cool, smooth surface of the tomb, a stark realization dawns on me—I feel utterly small against the backdrop of such monumental history. This place, with its profound connections to a past so grand and mysterious, seems so far beyond the simple life I was raised for, meant only to be a wife, not a seeker of hidden truths.

Lifting my gaze, I find Diarmuid watching me. His expression is intense, as if he is trying to decipher my thoughts. In his eyes, there's a recognition of something more, an acknowledgment of the person I am beneath the surface.

Near the front of the tomb, under the shadowy glow, stands a nervous-looking man. His figure is silhouetted against the light, barely revealing the famous entrance stone, its presence a silent testament to the ages. I must remind myself to temper my excitement; I am here as an investigator, not as a tourist enamored by the allure of history.

"Have all the arrangements been made?" Diarmuid's voice breaks the tension, directed at the man who looks like he wishes he were anywhere but here.

"Yes," the man replies, his voice barely a whisper. "I've called off the security guards who usually patrol at night." His eyes dart nervously toward the equipment Diarmuid has brought, the implication of our intentions weighing heavily on him.

Without wasting another moment, he leads us through the light bathing the entrance, into the heart of the tomb. The interior is illuminated by strategically placed artificial lights, designed to be invisible from the outside, casting eerie shadows on the ancient walls. As we step inside, the air shifts, cooler and somehow more alive with whispered secrets of millennia. My breath catches in my throat, the weight of what we might discover pressing down on me with exhilarating fear.

The familiar coolness of the stone, the earthy scent of the soil mixed with ancient dust, and the peculiar acoustics that amplify our every whisper remind me of my girlhood explorations, me an ignorant yet fascinated child.

Now, with knowledge as my guide, the enormity of the tomb's history wraps around me, stirring a blend of reverence and excitement. This isn't just a return; it's a journey to unearth secrets that have whispered through these stones for centuries.

I'm brought back to the present by Diarmuid's gesture, a nod that thrusts me into a role I hadn't anticipated tonight. With everyone's eyes on me, I assume the mantle of leadership, feeling a surge of responsibility as I instruct our guide. "Take us to the tunnel discovered by O'Kelly."

The guide stops, turns; his face is a mix of surprise and caution. "The tunnel doesn't exist."

My response is immediate, my voice firm with the weight of research. "In 1893, Captain Henry Keogh reported the existence of a tunnel on the immediate right upon entrance to the tomb. O'Kelly felt that the tunnel might be connected to an older mound that was made here before Newgrange."

There's a moment of tense silence before the guide replies, "That tunnel is narrow and dangerous. It is also blocked."

A flicker of frustration crosses Diarmuid's face, mirrored by a sense of urgency in Niamh's eyes. I step closer to the guide, lowering my voice to a persuasive whisper. "We've come a long way based on solid research. There's history here that hasn't been fully explored, and we believe it's crucial. Can you help us access it?"

The guide looks between us, the weight of our determination pressing against his concerns. He hesitates, then nods reluctantly. "I can take you to where the entrance is, but we've sealed it for safety. You can see it, but going through it isn't possible without proper clearance and preparation."

"Show me," I say, a note of determination cutting through the uncertainty that ripples beneath my words. Nerves bubble in my stomach, a turbulent mix of excitement and fear. If I'm wrong about this, I'll not only embarrass myself in front of this reluctant guide but also in front of Diarmuid. When we first met, his opinion barely mattered to me, but now, things have changed significantly. He cares about me, genuinely, and I find myself caring about his thoughts and feelings in return. Love, I realize, is both a blessing and a burden.

The guide leads us to a pillar just to the right of the exit. Diarmuid, sensing the shift in momentum, drops his bag and quickly distributes flashlights among us before picking it back up. Behind the pillar, barely noticeable unless you're looking for it, is a narrow opening—a tunnel that disappears into the darkness at a sharp angle.

It's daunting, smaller than the main passage, requiring us to move sideways to navigate through it. I take a deep breath, preparing myself for the cramped, claustrophobic journey ahead.

I thank the man with a nod.

"Keep watch outside, ensuring no one comes to interrupt our exploration." Diarmuid, ever vigilant, instructs the man. It feels like there is a moment of uncertainty in the man's posture before he dips his head in response and leaves.

We watch the man leave, and once he is out of sight, Diarmuid speaks. "That could lead to nowhere." His voice is tinged with concern as he eyes the narrow entrance.

"I know," I reply, trying to sound more confident than I feel. The need to know what lies ahead of us is so much stronger than anything I had ever felt. It's like a thirst for water. I need to take a drink.

"I'm not losing you," he asserts; the protective edge in his voice makes my heart skip.

I suppress a smile. "Then follow me," I say, meeting his gaze. "Make sure that if I go too far, you can bring me back."

Niamh, who has been quietly supportive until now, steps forward, her flashlight in hand. "What can I do?" she asks. Her voice conveys her eagerness to help, yet carries an undercurrent that she wants to be anywhere but in these confining tunnels.

"Stay out here in case someone needs to be called to get both of us." Diarmuid's voice is firm, his decision clear, as he addresses Niamh. He then drops the tools beside him, readying to drag them along as we move forward. It's a practical solution, given the constrained space and the need to keep our hands free.

I start into the tunnel, taking a few deep breaths to prepare myself—it might be my last chance for a while to breathe this freely. The passage is narrow, forcing me to move in an odd, sideways shuffle. I slide one arm along the wall while lifting the other ahead, holding the flashlight high to illuminate the path above. It's an awkward dance, and despite the seriousness of our quest, I can't help but let out a laugh. The sound echoes weirdly in the tight space, bouncing back at me from the cold, unyielding stone.

"Something you want to share?" Diarmuid asks.

I imagine Diarmuid behind me, likely mirroring my strange gait, and the thought makes me wish I could see him. The tunnel is constrictive, the stone cold against my chest and back as I press forward so looking back isn't an option. "No," I say, the laughter draining as quickly as the air from my body.

It doesn't take long before we reach what appears to be the end. Just as Captain Henry Keogh had reported, a pile of rocks and debris blocks further progress. The sight is disheartening, a physical barrier to both our path and my hopes.

"Blocked?" Diarmuid's voice carries a mix of resignation and inquiry.

"Blocked," I confirm, the word heavy and final.

"Good. This is already more than I wanted to do. Let's get out," Diarmuid says, his tone suggesting relief, perhaps a desire to retreat from the claustrophobic confines of this hidden passage.

But frustration wells up within me. I was so certain this was the place. It had to be. The clues, my research, everything pointed here. How could it just end like this? No, something in me refuses to accept this dead end as the conclusion of our search. My mind races, reviewing every piece of evidence, every historical account that led us here.

As I stretch my arm forward, fingers probing the cold, rough surface, they catch on something unexpected—a recess hidden in the wall. Excitement surges through me as I grip the corner of the stone and pull, maneuvering my body around what turns out to be a corner cleverly disguised by shadows and the limited light of earlier explorers.

Behind me, Diarmuid curses, his voice strained with effort and concern. It takes a few tense moments of wiggling and pushing, but finally, I manage to squeeze past the tight corner.

Relief washes over me as I find the tunnel opening up into a larger chamber—space that feels untouched, where the air holds the weight of undisturbed centuries.

"I know, I know. That was a lot, but look at this, Diarmuid," I call out as he follows, his breath heavy from exertion.

The chamber beyond is astonishing—a continuation of the swirl and diamond designs that mark the exterior of Newgrange, but here, added to them, are shapes of stars woven into the patterns. The designs remind me of Van Gogh's *The Starry Night*, with their dynamic, swirling energy that seems to pulse with life. Yet, these carvings are both natural and man-made, crafted with a precision that suggests both artistic flair and ceremonial importance. We leave the cavern and enter another tunnel.

Together, we follow the tunnel as it winds deeper into the earth. Our flashlights sweep over the walls, illuminating the ancient artwork until they finally fall upon a wall that rises abruptly in front of us. It's another apparent dead end, but a tiny opening in the wall catches our attention.

I step closer, heart pounding with the thrill of discovery and the fear of another barrier. It's then I notice something—a small carving beside the opening, so easy to overlook in our initial dismay. It's a crown etched into the palm of a raised hand.

"A crown in the hand," I whisper, tracing the lines with a finger, feeling the chisel marks left by some ancient artisan. The symbol resonates with power and mystery, and my mind races with the possibilities of its meaning.

"Diarmuid…" I say, my voice heavy with a mix of anticipation and anxiety.

"I know." His response is terse, reflecting his reluctance. He understands the potential of what we might uncover, but his concern for our safety weighs heavily on him.

I persist, fueled by the enormity of our discovery. "If we can trace any of the names in the tomb, any possible council members, then we can find their descendants. We can find the people who are above Victor." The gravity of our mission, the potential to unravel a hidden lineage of power, strengthens my resolve.

The plan remains unchanged. I take the lead, my left arm extended to feel my way, my right arm holding the flashlight overhead to guide our path through the narrow, constricting tunnel. The cold, earthen walls press against me from both sides, a constant reminder of the confining space that envelops us.

As I move forward, the tunnel seems to stretch endlessly ahead. I'm squeezing through the tightest spots, pressing against the damp soil, pushing forward with every bit of strength I have. Then, abruptly, a deep rumbling sound echoes behind me. My heart skips a beat. The flashlight is knocked from my grasp, clattering away into darkness. A moment later, Diarmuid's light vanishes too.

I am plunged into total darkness.

Panic claws at me as I try to squirm backward, only to be met with a solid wall that wasn't there before. The realization hits me hard—I'm trapped, separated from Diarmuid by this sudden collapse.

And in this pitch-black solitude, a profound truth settles over me: I want to live. More than that, I need to know that Diarmuid is safe, that he survives this too.

But the wall is between us now, its thickness unknown, its permanence a new barrier to my desperate hopes. I have no way of knowing how close he was when the tunnel caved in. All I can do is stare into the oppressive blackness, my eyes useless in this void.

Tears escape me, born of fear and frustration, streaming down my cheeks as I stand trapped in the earth's cold grip. I fall to my knees and try and feel around the damp earth, searching for my flashlight. If I can find it, at least I will be able to see it.

But my palms run across old earth, and I'm imagining rats and bugs climbing everywhere. I push the thought aside and try to steady my breathing. When the air seems thinner, I stop moving and squeeze my eyes tightly.

"It's okay, you are fine. Diarmuid will get you." I say the words out loud for comfort, but they don't stem the fear that crashes like the waves of a raging sea.

After a while, I hear a pounding sound. It's hard to tell if it's coming from outside, a rescue attempt by Diarmuid, or merely the pounding of my own heart—or perhaps it's the ominous drums of an impending end.

The fear is too much, the exertion and stress overwhelming. The air seems to shrink to less and less as panic consumes me.

223

CHAPTER TWENTY-TWO

Diarmuid

I t happens suddenly, without warning. The narrowness of these underground passages is suffocating. For Selene, it's a tight squeeze, but for me, with my barrel chest, it feels almost impossible. This second tunnel is worse than the first, the walls closing in even tighter, making me acutely aware of the tons of earth pressing down from above.

Somewhere in my mind, a bitter thought flickers to life: the man from the Hands of Kings who oversees these tunnels now must be skinny as a rail. I push through the constricting space by imagining snapping that twig of a man in half. It brings a twisted smile to my lips.

I'm following Selene, watching her effortlessly slither through the gap in front of me. Every muscle in my body is tense, ready to snatch her back at the slightest hint of danger. I've left my tools back in the larger tunnel; there's simply no room to carry them here, not if I want to be ready to help her.

My breaths come in shallow bursts. The walls are too close, preventing me from taking a full breath. Just as I start to adjust, the unthinkable happens.

A loud crash echoes through the tunnel, and suddenly, Selene disappears from my view. At first, my brain can't process the change. I'm frozen, shock rooting me in place. But as the seconds tick by, fury replaces the shock.

Selene.

It wasn't stone that blocked my way. Instead, an ancient wooden door adorned with iron bands and studs lies where Selene once was. It looks like it belongs in a medieval castle, not a tunnel dating back to 3200 BC.

Panic claws at me, but I force it down. I wriggle backward, squeezing myself out into the slightly larger space of the previous tunnel. My flashlight sweeps frantically around as I try to gather my thoughts.

Think, Diarmuid, think.

I grab my tools, my hand landing on the pickaxe. A spike of worry shoots through me. What if she's just on the other side of the door? I can't just swing wildly. The cramped quarters wouldn't allow for it anyway. But I can't just do nothing.

I need to get to Selene.

I don't let myself think about the worst—that she might be

crushed, already gone. I can't afford those thoughts. They're a luxury I don't have. Selene is just on the other side of that door. She's alive. She has to be.

With a grunt of determination, I kick my flashlight back into the smaller tunnel. It clatters against the door and rebounds, casting its beam toward me, a spotlight for my grim task. I squeeze back through the gap, the walls pressing against me like a vise.

The pickaxe feels heavy in my hand as I position myself as best I can in the confined space. It's excruciating trying to swing it. I'm used to leveraging my whole body into this kind of work, but here I can only use my arms. The initial swings feel pitifully weak, the dull thuds of metal against wood echoing mockingly in the tight space.

I grit my teeth and let out a bellow, each strike growing more intense. Again and again, I hit the door. My muscles scream in protest, the effort drawing raw, primal sounds from deep within me. I can't lose her. I *won't* lose her.

When the wood finally starts to crack, something shifts inside me—a wild, desperate hope. Energy surges through my veins, and I drop the pickaxe, attacking the weakening barrier with my bare hands. Splinters dig into my flesh, drawing blood, but I barely feel the pain. I tear at the wood, pieces flying as I desperately carve a path to Selene.

Each chunk of wood I rip away brings me closer to her, each moment filled with a frantic, frenzied urgency.

I'm coming, Selene. Hold on.

I become something feral, driven by instinct and adrenaline.

Each swing and tear at the door is more desperate than the last. A drop of my blood splatters onto the lens of my flashlight, distorting the light with a crimson hue. More blood, my own, runs in rivulets down the battered door.

The wood finally starts to give way under the relentless assault. I'm ripping chunks from the door, hurling them into the larger tunnel with wild abandon. When I've cleared enough space, I kick the flashlight back into the larger tunnel to retrieve it, then dive back into the smaller one, driven by the need to reach Selene.

The flashlight's beam reveals Selene's crumpled form. She's curled up awkwardly, motionless, a sight that tightens my chest with a cold grip of fear. I reach in, and as I drag her out, my bloodied hand stains her clothes.

We're back in the larger tunnel now, the light from the flashlight flickering, barely illuminating the shadows. My voice cracks as I scream for her to wake up. In the distance, I hear Niamh calling, but I can't focus on that. Niamh is safe. Selene isn't.

Miraculously, Selene stirs under my frantic pleas. As soon as her eyes flutter open, my lips find hers, not in a kiss of passion, but of desperate relief. She cries, her tears mingling with the blood and dirt on her face, clutching the back of my neck as she pulls herself closer.

"I'm so sorry," she sobs between her tears.

I just hold her, rocking slightly, whispering assurances, waiting until her breathing steadies and her heartbeat calms. We stay like that, enveloped in the dim light, anchored by each other's presence.

Finally, she speaks, her voice small and strained. "That was a trap."

I nod, my voice a low rumble of anger and confirmation. "It was."

Tears well up in Selene's eyes, but she staunchly wipes them away before they can fall. Slowly, she pushes herself to a sitting position, her voice steady despite the ordeal.

"Well, we are back at square one."

We both stand, and I grab our backpack of supplies; the weight of it is a solid reminder of our grim reality. I'm not looking forward to navigating back through that first, cramped tunnel. As I adjust the load, a shovel shifts and clatters to the ground, the sound echoing oddly as it hits.

First, stone and earth, then a hollow thud, like wood.

We freeze, exchanging a look. When my flashlight beam catches her eyes, her expression shifts—the fear is gone, replaced by a familiar, resolute spark.

That's my girl.

Together, we cleared the dirt and grime from where the shovel fell, uncovering a wooden door embedded in the floor.

A trap door.

Opening it requires both of us straining against its weight, but the effort pays off. The beam of my flashlight reveals a long, descending tunnel and a very modern, very metal ladder leading downward.

This time, I take the lead, descending first into the unknown. The climb down is lengthy and tense, with just one source of light between us. When we finally reach the bottom, we find ourselves in a tunnel constructed of brick and concrete. It stretches out far longer than any we've encountered so far, and it's too well-built to be anywhere near as ancient as Newgrange.

"This isn't just a tunnel," I mutter, scanning the sturdy walls and the path ahead. "It's a passage, built for purpose, and far too modern for any simple historical site."

We come to another ladder. "I'll go first," I say. I start to climb and push the trap door above my head. It opens easily and that makes me suspicious.

As we emerge from the ladder into the simplicity of the house above, the contrast is stark. The space is a modest, all-in-one room—living room, bedroom, and kitchen—coated with a thick layer of undisturbed dust. Sunlight filters through lace curtains, casting intricate shadows on the untouched surfaces. Night has gone since we arrived, and now morning has arrived. The air is thick with the mustiness of disuse.

I walk over to the kitchen sink, peering out the window. In the distance, Newgrange looms, majestic and isolated, separated from us by the shimmering ribbon of the River Boyne. The realization hits me hard—the tunnel went under the river.

Selene moves to my side, her presence a comforting constant. She's pondering, trying to connect the dots.

"I don't understand. So, I was right? Newgrange is still used by the Kings?" Her voice is a mix of disbelief and validation.

My hand tightens around the flashlight, my eyes fixed on the ancient tomb across the water. "You are right that it is used by the Kings," I acknowledge, "but it isn't used as a grave."

She turns to face me, confusion etched across her features. "What is the point of all of this, then?" Selene's eyes narrow, processing the harsh truth as it dawns on her. "Why go through all of that?" Her voice betrays a mix of curiosity and outrage, seeking to understand the depth of the deceit we've uncovered.

I lean against the cold kitchen counter, my mind racing as I piece together the motives behind the elaborate scheme. "Because Victor is a liar. The cult is fake," I state flatly, the bitterness in my voice as palpable as the dust in the air.

"The Hands of Kings—they've built this mythology, this mystique around Newgrange and their so-called ancient practices. But it's all a front," I continue, my hand sweeping across the room, gesturing to the ordinary setting that belied the extraordinary secrets hidden just beneath.

Selene steps closer, her determination mirroring mine. "So, they create a narrative, lure in the curious, the scholars, those who get too close to the truth, and then..." Her voice trails off, not needing to finish the thought.

"Exactly," I nod grimly. "It's a trap. An elaborate, well-crafted trap designed to protect their real activities. Whatever they are really up to, it's worth the effort to them to stage all this—stage accidents or disappearances for anyone who might expose them."

Selene crosses her arms, her brain visibly turning over the implications. "This house, the tunnel, the false leads in Michael's office—it's all just part of a larger scheme to mislead and eliminate threats."

I look back out the window at the distant view of Newgrange, feeling the pieces click into place. "And we've just walked straight into it. But now that we know, we have a chance to turn the tables. We need to find out what they're really hiding and expose it."

Selene nods, her eyes reflecting a fiery resolve. "Let's start by going back over everything we've seen and collected. There must be a clue somewhere that leads to their real operations."

CHAPTER TWENTY-THREE

Amira

I'm used to horrible people wearing pretty masks. My mother, for instance, spent most of her days hiding in our continuously rotting mansion, yet she acted like a different person in public. Her smile was wide and dazzling, her touch gentle as she guided me around rooms filled with people who were important in their own circles but meant nothing at all to me.

The Hands of Kings reminds me of her. Early December brings light dustings of snow and nights dark and cold. Another event, another way for the Kings to wear those pretty masks. Like the Diners of Influence dinner a few months ago, this one is open to the public. This event is meant to show the best side of the cult, to garner support from powerful players in Ireland.

But it's all a lie.

I sit in the corner of a sitting room under a painting of the Furies of Greek mythology—three sisters tasked with bringing justice to the world of men. The captain had named the vessel Alecto, after the fiercest of the three sisters. I can't help but feel a connection to that name, to that fierce justice that seems so distant from the reality I'm living in.

A majority of the guests have gathered outside to watch the lights of Dublin float by as the super yacht glides along the River Liffey. I stay below decks, away from the spectacle.

Out of nowhere, Wolf hits my arm with the back of his hand and points to the bar area. The interior of the super yacht looks more like a spaceship than a vessel meant for the sea. When I first came on board, I didn't even realize that some of the cabinets were cabinets at all. Only an hour into our cruise, I know exactly where all the goodies are. Wolf has already taken inventory, of course.

I pour him another glass of scotch, the amber liquid reflecting the sleek, modern lines of the bar.

"They made me stand on the docks," Wolf mutters, his voice low and bitter.

He doesn't need to tell me this; I was there. I saw the way he seethed, struggling with being a Duke under his King cousins. This latest demotion only added to his fury. As a Marquess, he couldn't board the ship until every King and Duke was on board. Diarmuid O'Sullivan took his damn time arriving with his two remaining Brides.

The top deck has been supplied with streaming lights and

heaters, making the river cruise bearable in the winter chill. The Kings never do anything in the usual way. I can hear the murmurs of the people who come in to use the bathrooms, talking about how beautiful it is upstairs. I imagine the scene: twinkling lights reflecting off the water, the skyline of Dublin a glittering backdrop.

It's a shame I'm stuck down here. My eyes flick back to Alecto as Wolf continues to mumble to himself. The fierceness in the Fury's eyes and the conviction in her pose draw me in, a silent reminder of the justice that feels so far out of reach.

"They will never respect you, Wolf," I say, my voice cold and devoid of emotion. I don't even look at him when I say it. Part of me is afraid to. Another part of me knows it will infuriate him more if I disrespect him by not making eye contact.

Wolf snatches my hair from across the table and twists it. The burn along my scalp is instant, but I have become accustomed to pain. His grip twists further, forcing me to look at him. "What the fuck did you just say?" he growls, his face inches from mine.

Calluses don't just form on the skin; they most often form on the heart. Abuse disguising itself as love has been my companion for my entire life. Wolf is just the final crack that broke the dam. After the waters receded, I was left empty. There's no Amira left to hurt.

I meet his eyes, the fury in them not surprising me anymore. "Look what they've done to you, my love."

The words "my love" are a lie to a liar. Wolf's grip on my hair loosens, and he leans back into his chair. Calmly, in an almost motherly fashion, I reach into my bag and retrieve a small bag of white powder. I get out a credit card, pour some powder on the tabletop, and use the card to cut it into lines.

"Take your medicine, Wolf," I say, pushing the lines toward him.

He stares at me for a moment, then leans forward, his expression softening. The anger in his eyes is replaced by a hollow need. Without a word, he takes the rolled-up bill I hand him and snorts a line. The transformation is almost immediate—his body relaxes, and the tension drains from his face.

I watch him, feeling a strange mix of pity and contempt. This man, so powerful and so broken, is reduced to seeking solace in a bag of powder. I should feel something—anger, sadness, anything—but there's nothing left. I'm empty, a shell that goes through the motions without any real connection to the world around me.

One line isn't enough. He's already had plenty to drink, but I need to push him over the edge. Push him like he's pushed me. I prep another line for him, steadying my hands as I continue talking.

"Your father was the head of the O'Sullivan family," I say, my voice calm and controlled.

Wolf nods, eyes glazing over. "He was."

"Who is the head of the family now?"

His hand lashes out, slapping me hard. One of his rings drags across my cheek, leaving a stinging line of pain. But nothing erupts within me. There's a calmness, a cold clarity that processes the information and urges me forward.

"Diarmuid is the son of a man who tried to leave the order," I continue, my voice unwavering. "He should have been ineligible."

"I fucking know that," Wolf snarls and snorts the second line. His movements are becoming sluggish, his eyes unfocused.

I look up at Alecto again, gathering my courage. The fierce justice in her eyes fuels me. Suddenly, I launch across the table, grabbing Wolf by the hair, twisting it. This time, I make him look at me.

Between the drugs and the alcohol, his reflexes are slow. He grits his teeth and starts cursing at me. One of his fists connects with my jaw, but I don't flinch. My teeth are gritted with wild, animalistic fury as I speak.

"Victor has done this to you. He has broken the rules just so you will lose. You will always lose with him around, Wolf. Always. He didn't give a fuck about your father. In fact, it looks like he may have gotten rid of him just to take your inheritance from you."

Wolf's eyes widen as the realization dawns on him, like a predator preparing for a hunt. I lean closer, my grip on his hair tightening.

"He is right upstairs, Wolf. Surrounded by people who cannot protect him. On a ship in the middle of the river. He won't get away."

For a moment, there is silence between us, thick and heavy. Wolf's breathing is ragged, his eyes wild with a mixture of rage and desperation. I let go of his hair and step back, watching as he processes what I've told him.

"Upstairs," he repeats, his voice barely a whisper.

I nod, feeling a cold satisfaction settle in my chest. "Yes. This is your chance, Wolf. To take back what's yours. To show them all that you are not to be underestimated." His gaze flickers like he's considering my words, but I don't want to leave any room for error.

I kiss him deeply, more lovingly than I intended. Oh, the things we sacrifice when sealing deals.

"We could rule it all, Wolf. Only one old man stands in our way," I whisper against his lips.

Wolf kisses me back furiously, painfully. His hands grip me with a desperation that borders on violence. He stands up, draws his pistol, and starts up the stairs to the deck. I watch him go, my heart pounding in my chest.

I know I can't follow him directly. I need to maintain the illusion that I'm not part of this. I opt to go further down the deck before making my way topside.

As I navigate the sleek, modern corridors of the super yacht, the sounds of merriment above grow louder. I pause at the base of a different staircase, taking a deep breath to steady myself. I can't afford to make any mistakes.

I emerge on the upper deck a few moments later, slipping into the crowd unnoticed. The guests are all gathered, admiring the view of Dublin's lights reflecting off the River Liffey. I spot Wolf on the other side of the deck, his eyes fixed on Victor, who is surrounded by sycophants, laughing and toasting as if nothing in the world could touch him.

I position myself near the edge of the crowd, feigning interest in the view. The cold night air bites at my skin, but I barely feel it. My attention is wholly on Wolf as he moves closer to Victor.

"Such a beautiful night," a woman next to me remarks. I

nod absently, not really hearing her. I've allowed my hair to fall across my damaged cheek in hopes of concealing the mark that Wolf left on me.

I watch Wolf move toward Victor. No one seems to notice him, like the ghost he is.

Excitement bubbles up inside me. I'm feeling something for the first time in a long time.

I have played my part well, and now it's time to see how the pieces fall. The masks are off, and the real game has just begun.

CHAPTER TWENTY-FOUR

Diarmuid

The night is cold, typical of early December in Dublin. I shiver, feeling the chill seep through my coat. I want to keep both of them close to me, to use my body to make sure they stay warm. Every instinct in me screams to get them out of this, to take them somewhere private and make sure they are warm and safe. But the circus had begun. It's time for the King to be a Jester, to paint a smile on my face and act like the friendly neighborhood assassin.

Cocktails are served. Some cold. Some warm. It's a night of pretentious elbow-rubbing among the kind of people who make decisions that affect millions of lives over a bet and a handshake. People who feed off the souls of those below them.

Selene and Niamh play their parts so well, smiling at all the fake-friendly faces. I nod and greet everyone as I move through the crowd. We've all been given drinks; I leave mine on a nearby table as I greet people. I don't intend to drink tonight. I'm ready to keep moving when Niamh pauses, looking out over the railing of the boat. The city lights twinkle, and it is a beautiful sight, but I'm not here for sightseeing.

She untangles her arm from mine. "I want to get a closer look." She smiles up at me and with excitement bubbling in her gaze.

"Stay in sight," I say, not wanting her to go.

"Hello, Mr.O'Sullivan." The voice cuts through the air, and I turn to an early arrival, a lady wrapped in a gold dress that appears to have been dipped in the rare metal.

She waves a hand dripping in more of the jewelry. Gold isn't native to our planet; it comes from fallen stars that rained down on Earth. It's a precious metal but one flaunted by the rich.

"You look wonderful," I say, not knowing the lady's name.

She giggles, her face unmoving, and glances at Selene, who seems to tighten her hold on my arm. "Not as stunning as this beauty on your arm." She smiles at Selene, but her gaze is assessing. I have the overwhelming need to step in front of Selene and block her. She's too pure for this world.

I glance around the deck, my eyes searching for any sign of Niamh. She wandered off to look at the city lights. I can't blame her; anything would be more appealing than this crowd. Yet, I had told her to stay in sight.

"Thank you," Selene says, drawing my attention back to her, and I really look at Selene.

Sleek, beautiful Selene, with steel blue eyes that seem to pierce through me and read me in a way I have never been seen before. She moves closer, dangerously close—the kind of close where I don't trust my mind to slow down my body.

"Well, I shall leave you both to it; young love is such a beautiful thing." She waves her hand in the air, and I nod with a small smile as she departs.

Once the lady has left, Selene leans into me and whispers, "I can't wait to go home."

That stirs the desire in me. Yes. Home. The place where I only have to be Diarmuid, not the holder of the myriad of duties someone like me holds outside those sacred walls. I can almost feel the warmth of the fire, the comfort of being just myself, without the masks and charades.

I'm getting lost in her eyes, in the promise of escape they hold, when I hear the gunshot.

My heart lurches. There's nowhere to run, not on the river. As big as this super yacht is, it's still a relatively small place. Fuck. A gun. Here. With nowhere to go.

I need to find the source of the threat. I place Selene behind my back as I quickly scan the chaotic crowd for Niamh. But it's impossible with people running in all directions. I push through the crowd and move toward the sound.

The crowd is a frenzied mess, pushing away from the source

of the noise. I push through the useless gawkers, my mind racing. I need to get to the scene before things get worse.

I break through the throng and see Wolf standing in front of me. Across from both of us is Victor. Wolf has a gun pointed at the Hand. The crowd falls silent, and I can see Wolf's hand shake; he's unable to stand still. He isn't himself. He's worse than himself. He's volatile.

"You have the answers. You always have the fucking answers. All this time. Nothing. You don't fucking care. You don't care what they fucking did to him." Wolf screams at Victor, his voice raw and broken with each word.

Victor stares at Wolf as if he's an interesting painting instead of a coked-up drunk with a gun pointed at him. His calmness is infuriating, that far-off stare making it seem like he's above all this chaos.

"And since you know the answers and nothing has been done, that means you are fucking fine with what happened." Wolf's voice cracks, the anger giving way to anguish.

Still, no reaction from Victor. Just that cold, detached look. Then, subtly, Victor's eyes flick to mine and back to Wolf. A tiny but powerful command. The kind of command that means life or death. The command that tells me to use all my training to take down Wolf.

My heart pounds as I process what Victor asks. This isn't a mission to be completed in the depth of night, away from the public. We are surrounded by people. Surrounded by those who will know exactly what I am when I make my move. Victor is willing to expose his greatest weapon to save his own life.

This could be dangerous for me. A hitman whose face is known is useless. Victor could dispose of me. Or he could protect me out of gratitude. Gratitude. It's been drilled into my head since childhood. I need to be grateful for everything the Kings have provided for me. I need to be grateful for being a King, not a Baron. Not a Page.

But none of this had been given to me. None of this had been a gift. It had been earned through blood, most of it my own.

Wolf killing Victor would take away the satisfaction of me doing it myself, but how glorious would it be? Victor right in front of me, relying on his kicked, abused dog to protect him, and that dog letting the bullet go right through his skull.

Fuck satisfaction. Sometimes you must sacrifice that to get what you want. And I want Victor dead.

I take a step back, trying to signal to Victor that his guard dog is backing down, that he is going to die tonight. I fully intend to commit to this decision until I notice a face peering over Victor's shoulder.

Amira.

The one I lost. The one who couldn't trust me. Amira with the cold eyes, heavy makeup, and the misshapen lip.

But that's not what I remember about her. Her face was perfect. Doll-like. As I look closer, I notice how one of her eyes is swollen. The lip and the eye...how much is that makeup covering up?

What the fuck has Wolf done to her?

I move more by training and instinct than thought; the crowd parts easily. Wolf has his back to me; he's still shouting, so he doesn't see me coming. But, right there, at that very second, a subtle shift in Victor's gaze catches my attention—one that surprises me—relief flashes across his stone features.

My hand reaches out to Wolf, pushing the arm with the gun straight into the air. The gun goes off. Screams erupt around us as the gawking crowd scrambles for cover. Wolf turns toward me. I don't think but react. My forehead slams into his face. He staggers back from the impact, and I use the moment to knock the gun out of his hand, with one sleek high kick. It slides across the deck and disappears into the waters below. With the loss of his gun, Wolf grips his face, blood already pouring from his broken nose through his fingers.

He slowly lowers his hands and looks up at me, smiling through the blood, his white teeth looking predatory through the scarlet.

Wolf roars and rushes toward me. I easily twist him around, hooking my ankle behind his leg and sending him crashing to the ground. He spins quickly from his belly to his back, but I show no mercy.

I'm on him, and before my fist connects with his face, he grins at me again.

"Do your best!"

I cut off his laughter, ramming my fist into his mouth. His laughter returns loud and maniacal. Blood spews, and my fist comes up and down, over and over again, until he has nothing left to laugh about. Blood covers my knuckles, splattering on the crowd that can't get through the door to the interior fast enough. Each blow brings a grim satisfaction, a release of all the pent-up rage and frustration.

I don't think he can take much more, so I stop, but don't get off him. His laughter bubbles quickly, and my fist comes down one more time. Wolf isn't conquered, though. He springs, his mouth gaping, and his mouth covers my knuckles, his teeth sinking into my flesh. Pain shoots up my arm, sharp and hot. I grunt, trying to pull my hand free, but his grip is ironclad.

"Bastard!" I snarl, yanking my hand back and feeling the skin tear. Blood runs from the wound, mingling with his on my knuckles. I rear back, kicking him hard in the ribs, sending him sprawling.

But Wolf isn't human, not with the drugs coursing through his veins. Most men would have been knocked out by the blows to the head. With seemingly superhuman strength, Wolf rises and tries to wipe blood from his face, only to smear it across his cheek. He's a bloody mess.

He staggers, and I move toward him to grab him, but he reaches me, no longer feeble but fully with it. He grabs my arms and twists them to the side, his forehead colliding with my nose as he brings his face forward. The impact sends me sailing backward, and I'm the one on the ground.

Show no mercy! That's what happens when you let your guard down.

He roars as he rushes me, and I struggle to get to my feet. His foot connects with my face, and pain explodes across my vision. This time, it's my blood that splatters on the wooden deck.

He draws his leg back to kick me again. I reach out and grab his ankle and twist it until I hear something snap. His screams follow him all the way to the deck. Rage consumes me as my head rings from the kick.

I stand and sprint toward Wolf, who manages to get to his feet. He retreats, limping on a damaged ankle that has to hurt like a bitch. But nothing slows him down as he races down the side of the yacht, his eyes wild and frantic.

People scream and jump out of his way.

"Move!" he roars. No one intervenes, and I know it's because Victor wants a show. Victor has only given me the order to take down Wolf, and no one else would dare cross him.

Up ahead, Niamh scrambles at a door that seems to be locked. There is fear in her face, and it propels me forward with a renewed sense of urgency.

I grab a fire extinguisher from the wall and stride purposefully toward Wolf, who has slowed down, his left leg trailing behind his body. He might not feel the pain, but his body can't take the abuse to his broken ankle.

I reach him and raise the fire extinguisher. It crashes down on the back of his head, and he staggers but doesn't fall.

What the fuck did he take?

I won't stop. I raise the fire extinguisher again, and it comes down with a sickening crack of his skull. He blinks hard, losing consciousness. He is beaten. He knows it. He pivots toward me, raising his hands like I will show mercy.

"You have nowhere to go!" I growl, still holding the fire extinguisher. One more blow would surely end him. Blood pours from the back of his head down the side of his neck. If we stand here long enough, he will bleed out.

Wolf is covered in blood, his body barely staying upright .

"Stand down." I give him a final warning.

Wolf does what every cornered animal would do. With the last of his strength, he rushes toward Niamh, grabs her around the waist, lifts her, and takes both of them over the railing.

Into the darkness. Into the roaring cold water of the Irish sea.

Fear grips me by the throat. The fire extinguisher bounces off the wooden deck in silence as I watch them being dragged under and swallowed by the unforgiving sea.

CHAPTER TWENTY-FIVE

Nimah

The ironic part about being dragged into the depths of this icy hell is that I had just finished talking to a priest. If only I had known, I could have had my last rites read to me. Diarmuid had performed his public duties diligently, sweeping through the decks with both Selene and me. Everyone we met was kind and courteous, full of small nods and compliments about how beautiful we both looked.

It became a game for me to try to figure out who was part of the cult and who was being used by the cult. But it was impossible to tell. Sometimes, the wolves do fool the sheep. Everyone looked like someone's mother or father. No one struck me as a killer.

I'd become much more interested in watching the lights shimmer off the river as we floated by the various Dublin neighborhoods. Diarmuid told me to stay close and to stay in his line of sight. I never got to answer as he was swept away by a woman who looked expensive; he and Selene became engrossed in their conversation. I was forgotten so quickly. But ever since I accepted the reality of Selene and Diarmuid, a sense of relief has washed over me.

The competition is over. Selene won, but I can't be bitter about it. Selene challenged Diarmuid, mentally sparred with him. I had been too timid, too reserved. Perhaps I will perform better next time.

I have no doubt there will be a next time. I have to continue with this folly. For Ella. To protect her. Maybe it would help to be a bit more like Amira.

Someone comes to the railing beside me, settling themselves next to me. When I look up, I don't quite remember who the man is, but I know I've seen him before. It takes a while, but I remember him as the priest I saw with Selene during the Diners of Influence event.

"Father, I am surprised to see you here," I say, my voice tinged with curiosity and a hint of wariness. Could he be a wolf in sheep's clothing? Victor was a high priest, and he was the worst of them all, so I keep my guard up.

The priest clears his throat and turns to me with a gentle smile. "I have surprised myself by being here, miss. I beg your pardon for the intrusion; you seem to have been very much consumed by your thoughts."

I blink, pulled from my reverie. "Water tends to make me think," I reply, glancing back at the shimmering river. The smell always draws me closer, like something under the murky water calls to me.

"Because water is calming and reflective," he says, nodding thoughtfully.

"What have you come here to reflect on?" I ask, genuinely curious now. I know what drew me to the water, but I wonder what has brought him over.

"All of this, really. I had received invitations to these events for years, but I never found myself wanting to attend them. That is, until Diarmuid O'Sullivan appeared at my church." He pauses, his gaze steady on mine. "I know the secret, Niamh."

My heart skips a beat. "I don't know what you mean," I say, trying to keep my voice steady, but my mind races. There are so many secrets, and I'm not even sure which one he refers to.

He leans in slightly, his voice lowering, he glances left to right before he speaks. "I know what all of this is. Diarmuid. The order. Victor."

I glance back into the water. My mind goes to Rian. He had found out all their secrets, too, and he's six feet under. I owe nothing to the priest, but a sense of decency has me turning to him.

"For your own sake, I would be satisfied with the knowledge you have," I say, my voice low and urgent. "Horrible things happen to people who pry."

Father Isaac looks at me, his expression calm but serious. "I know this, which is why I want you to know that if anything happens to you, you have a place to go. For safety."

I furrow my brow, confusion and suspicion mingling in my mind. "Why are you offering me this?"

He smiles faintly, a touch of sadness in his eyes. "You don't belong in this world, miss."

"I think that's how everyone may start out. But, in time, it pulls us all in, just like the water."

The sadness doesn't leave his gaze. "My church can be a safe haven if you ever find yourself in need." With a nod toward me, he turns and walks inside, using a door not far from where we stood.

It's funny as I ponder his words. I have nowhere to turn to if I needed help. I hope I never have to go to him, but maybe one day, having him as a contact will be useful.

My heart lurches as a loud bang seems to silence the night before the world before me explodes into madness. People rush past; a woman bounces off me, and I grip the railing to stop myself from sailing over the edge.

My heart leaps into my throat as another loud bang fills the air. My brain catches up with the noise I just heard. It was a second gunshot.

Diarmuid had told me to go inside if anything was to happen. He had warned Selene and me to get to safety before we arrived at the event. At the time I had thought about what could happen on a yacht full of people.

I race with the crowd but glance over my shoulder. Through

gaps in the masses of people, I see Diarmuid and Wolf fighting violently. I pause and nearly get trampled again. A man slams into me, and I fall along the deck, gripping the rail. Another man stops and helps me to my feet.

"You need to run." His face is close to mine, and then he's gone. I spin, losing any sense of what's happening. I can't see Selene. I scream her name over the panicked people, hunting for her large blue gown. She should be easy to spot, but I don't see her. She must have gotten to safety already. I start moving with the dwindling crowd. The door is closed, but a man races through and slams it behind him.

"Wait!" I scream and yank the handle, but it's locked from the inside. The man's face appears through a small oval window. "Open the door!" I beg.

He disappears and I spin, plastering my back to the door.

I race to the nearest door, only to find it locked, too. Panic rises in my chest. The next deck is too high to climb. I am trapped.

Suddenly, Wolf and Diarmuid come into view, grappling with each other, their movements a blur of violence. I try to stay out of the way, but my feet betray me. I trip on someone's bag that must have fallen through their panic to get away. The strap trips me, and I fall against the railing, looking down at the raging sea once again. I quickly right myself.

Wolf is between Diarmuid and me, his face a mask of rage and determination as he sees me. I'm frozen, my limbs useless. And then, the unthinkable happens.

He grabs me and, in a terrifyingly swift motion, hurls us both over the railing into the churning waters below.

At first, I feel nothing. The water breaks around us, and for a moment, I am suspended above the darkness of the deeper river. I am nothing. I am everything. Time itself halts.

Then, it all hits at once.

Pain beyond anything I have ever experienced seizes me. My skin tightens all over my body so intensely that the water burns like fire. It is inescapable. It is everywhere. The cold is so intense it feels like my blood freezes solid. I try to scream, but the icy water fills my mouth and my lungs. Panic and agony intertwine, blurring the edges of my consciousness.

I struggle, my limbs flailing, but the current pulls me down, deeper into the dark abyss. My thoughts scatter, memories of Ella—smiling at me, teasing me, watching her sleep—assault my mind. Then Diarmuid's face appears, the first time I met him, and the images mesh together. Everything I'm fighting for flickers and fades. All that remains is the primal, overwhelming need to survive.

But survival seems impossible in this icy hell.

I try to kick toward the surface, but the shoes strapped to my feet make my kicks sluggish, useless. Desperation fuels me as I reach down, fumbling to unstrap them. Finally, I kick them off, watching them disappear into the darkness. My dress restricts my movements, and the cold gnaws at my bones, but I am strong.

I am the woman who dreams of conquering the North Sea,

the English Channel, the Tsugaru Channel. This is a short swim. Easily manageable.

I am strong.

With my arms extended, I start long, powerful strokes toward the surface. Hope surges within me, but then something grabs me, yanking me back into the depths.

There's enough light from the ferry for me to see him—Wolf. And with him comes a cloud of blood, blinding me. He sinks, and he takes me with him.

His grip is strong, but I am stronger. On land, he would dominate me, but this is the water. This is where I am meant to be.

I am strong. Stronger than him, than his enmity.

I deliver a few powerful, well-centered kicks, and his grip loosens. He continues to fall into the darkness, his eyes wide with shock and fury.

I look up, seeing the shimmering light above me. I just need to get to it. My muscles are starting to seize from the cold, the first stage of hypothermia. Wolf dragged me down further than I am comfortable being, but I am strong. I can do this. That shimmering light. I just need to reach it. Everything will be fine once I reach it.

Each stroke is a test of my will. My muscles scream in protest, but I push through the pain. The light gets closer. I can see the surface now, tantalizingly close. My lungs burn for air, and my vision starts to blur around the edges.

Just a little more. Just a few more strokes. I grit my teeth, channeling every ounce of strength I have left. The cold is relentless, but so am I.

I am so close. My strength is nearly gone, but I extend my hand, and my fingertips break the surface. For a fleeting moment, I touch the air, taste the promise of life above.

But I can't do it. I'm not strong enough.

As my strength gives out, I begin to fall back into the darkness. I wonder if Sofia will be on the other side. Will she be able to tell me what happened to her? Maybe I could contact Selene from the other side. I hope Selene ends up happy in this world; it seems like an impossible task. I think of Ella, with her profile that looks so much like a grown woman. I hope that whatever I did in this cult was enough to ensure that Ella would never have to go through what I have gone through, never have to know this fear.

Fear. I thought I would be more scared in this moment. But I'm not.

Suddenly, a pair of arms are around me. I break the surface, gasping. Diarmuid has saved me. Selene screams. I can hear Victor's voice giving commands.

Diarmuid's voice is urgent and soothing in my ear. "Hold on, Niamh. You've done so well. I'm so proud of you. Just hold on."

I am so weak. I know that I am saved, but sleep seems like such a gift. Especially with how beautifully the lights are shimmering on the water. The cold no longer feels like pain, but like a blanket pulling me into peaceful oblivion.

"Stay with me, Niamh," Diarmuid's voice insists, a lifeline pulling me back. His grip is strong, his determination palpable.

I blink, fighting the overwhelming urge to close my eyes. The lights blur, and Selene's frantic face is above me. "Niamh! Stay awake!" she screams, her voice cutting through the haze.

Victor's commands are a distant roar, but they ground me in reality. I focus on Diarmuid's voice, his words. "I'm so proud of you," he repeats, his tone steady and reassuring.

My vision narrows, the darkness at the edges creeping closer. But I hold on. For Diarmuid, for Selene, for Ella. I must stay awake. I must survive.

The world above the water is chaotic, but it's also filled with hope and life. I cling to that, to the shimmering lights and the warmth of Diarmuid's arms.

I want to tell Diarmuid I'm sorry. I'm so sorry. I'm not strong enough. The darkness consumes me. There is no flash of memories or a bright light. All there is darkness and cold.

CHAPTER TWENTY-SIX

Amira

The taxi ride back to Wolf's place fills me with a twisted sense of giddiness. I can't help but smile to myself. No one had searched for him. Diarmuid's beating had ensured he wouldn't survive the icy waters. A fate he deserved, I tell myself, trying to push away the lingering guilt.

The earlier drugs are wearing off, and I start to feel every bite and pinch of my broken skin from Wolf's recent abuse. My body aches, a constant reminder of the torment I've endured. I shift uncomfortably in the seat, wincing as the motion sends a jolt of pain through me.

"Almost there," the driver says, glancing at me through the

rearview mirror. I nod, my mind elsewhere, replaying the events that led to this moment. The rage in Wolf's eyes, the sickening sound of flesh meeting flesh, and then the water, the unforgiving water swallowing him up. Watching him go over the rail had filled me with so much joy.

I suppress a smile.

I bite my lip, trying to focus on something else, anything else to keep the laughter at bay. The city lights blur past the window, and I close my eyes, letting out a slow, shaky breath. I need to stay strong.

As we pull up to Wolf's place, a shiver runs down my spine. The driver stops, and I fumble for the fare, my hands trembling. I catch a glimpse of my reflection in the window, battered and bruised, but there's a spark of defiance in my eyes. I can do this. I have to.

"Thanks," I mutter to the driver, pushing the door open and stepping out. The cold air hits me, stinging my cuts and bruises. I square my shoulders and head towards the entrance, each step a painful reminder of what I've been through. But I'm still standing. And as long as I'm standing, there's hope.

My legs are unsteady but determined. I make my way to his office, the path familiar despite the haze of pain and drugs. I know exactly where he keeps his stash.

Once inside, I head straight to the hidden compartment behind the bookshelf. My fingers fumble for a moment before finding the small white bag. I pull it out, my hands trembling with anticipation.

With quick, practiced movements, I pour the contents onto the table and use my fingers to form large white lines.

I don't have anything else to use, so I bend down and sniff them off the table, the harsh chemical smell burning my nostrils. The instant the drug hits my system, a rush of euphoria washes over me. I throw my head back and laugh, the sound echoing in the empty office.

For a moment, the pain fades, replaced by a heady mix of relief and reckless abandon. The world around me blurs, and I am invincible, untouchable. I know it won't last, but right now, it's exactly what I need.

"Freedom!" I scream, not caring who hears me. This is my fucking domain now. The sound echoes through the empty halls, a declaration of my newfound power. I stride over to the bar and grab a bottle of whiskey, unscrewing the cap with a savage twist.

My eyes land on Wolf's desk, littered with plans and pictures of young women, reminders of his twisted control. With a wicked grin, I start pouring the liquor over everything, soaking the papers and photographs. The sight is so satisfying, all of his meticulous plans dissolving into a soggy mess.

When the bottle is empty, I don't hesitate. I smash it against the wall, the sound of shattering glass sending a thrill through me. I grab another bottle, my hands steady now with purpose. I take a swig, the burning liquid fueling my fire.

"I own this place now," I whisper to myself, feeling a surge of defiance. This is my moment, my revenge. Everything he built, everything he controlled—it's all mine to destroy. I take another drink, savoring the taste of rebellion and freedom.

I walk through the brothel, the sound of my heels clicking against the stone floor echoing in the empty halls. The bottle of fine whiskey in my hand—sloshes with each unsteady step. I stagger, but I keep moving. The chaos on the yacht made everyone forget me.

Alecto had rushed back to the pier after Niamh was pulled from the water. Thank God for the high society on that yacht; with their abundance of high-ranking medical professionals, they had rushed to Niamh's side as Diarmuid had frantically tried to pull her from the edge of death. Poor little ballerina Niamh was causing all sorts of worried brows and frantic whispers. She was still unconscious when I slipped into a cab and left. I wonder if it had been me dragged deep under, if anyone would have blinked, or would I, even now, be rotting at the bottom of the ocean with Wolf?

The fabric of my dress clings uncomfortably to my skin, catching on the open wounds. My thighs, my face, my entire body still ache from the damage Wolf inflicted on me. Every step is a reminder. But it will heal. Eventually, all wounds heal. He will never get to lay his hands on me again.

I take another swig from the whiskey bottle, feeling the burn down my throat. For the first time in a long time, I am in control of my own fate. I don't know what my cure is yet, but I will be the one to choose it. No more being forced into corners and cages.

The halls are eerily empty. Surely, no one here has heard about what happened yet. They don't know that Wolf is gone. Gone. The thought brings a twisted sense of satisfaction. Oh, ladies. It is only Amira who haunts these hallways now. I grin and run my hands along the walls, my finger catching on the edge of some ancient painting. I watch with satisfaction as it tilts and falls from the wall to crash on the ground behind me.

When the staff are around, they avoid me. They hate me. I can see it in their eyes, in the way they scatter like mice when I pass. But what they don't understand is that I was just as much a victim as they were.

I laugh bitterly to myself. Victim or not, I'm still standing. And for now, that's enough. I can't see the staff, but I know they hide like rats in their rooms. I don't want them here; I don't want to see their accusing gazes or hateful stares anymore. My steps grow more rushed, and a scream tears from my throat.

I scream and bang on doors, my voice raw and wild. "Get out! Everyone, get out!" I'm a madwoman, tearing through the rooms like a whirlwind. I fling open every door, tearing into each room and unleashing destruction on everything I touch. The maids look at me, stunned for a moment.

"Are you fucking deaf?! Get out!" Two scurry past me like the rats they are. Every picture on the wall I rip down, every chair I turn over, all of the bedding I rip free from the beds, knocking over lamps, and their meager possessions rain down on the floor.

I re-enter the hall and howl from the top of my lungs. "Get out, now!!!" Doors open, and maids with bent heads rush from their rooms. I laugh.

"Run! Run! That's all you can do now!!" Darkness overtakes me, and all I am is a symphony of rage and chaos.

The women scream in fear, their cries mingling with mine. But as for my screams, I don't know what they are. I'm not ready to slow down and figure out what I'm feeling. I just know that I hate this place. I hate every inch of this fucking place. I want to destroy it all. It doesn't exhaust me to tear each room apart; it drives me to do as much damage as I can. A lamp sails across the room and smashes through one of the closed windows. Glass rains down, and a breeze stirs the curtains.

I'm back in the hall, and I lift one of my heeled shoes and kick open the door to one of the love rooms. Pillows. Blankets. Beds. Hearts. All mocking facades of affection. There was no love here. There was never love here.

Taking another long drink from the whiskey bottle, I start piling pillows and blankets in the middle of the room. The fabric rustles with a sinister whisper, feeding my fury. I stagger to the fake fireplace against the wall and light the candles, each flame a spark of defiance. Laughing manically, I carefully walk back to my pile, setting the candles among the mass of fabric. I'm precise with the candles but careless with the junk I heap on top of them.

Before long, the pile begins to smoke. A vibrant orange flame catches, crackling and dancing. The sight only fuels my madness. I throw anything I can find into the growing inferno—sheets, cushions, even the gaudy heart-shaped decor. When I run out of objects, I take one last swig of the whiskey, the burn in my throat a match for the fire in my heart. With a defiant cry, I toss the bottle into the flames.

It explodes with a deafening roar, shards of glass scattering like deadly confetti. The far wall catches, the fire spreading rapidly, consuming everything in its path. The room transforms into an inferno, a chaotic symphony of destruction.

I stand there, watching the flames engulf the room, a twisted sense of satisfaction curling through me. This place, this lie, is burning down, and with it, a piece of my past. Let them hate me. Let them fear me. In this moment, I am free.

I'm laughing, tears streaming down my cheeks, my eyeliner running in dark streaks. There are still people here. I bang on the remaining doors, yelling at everyone to leave. "Get out! Get out now!" But my screams are unnecessary; they're already running from me, their terror palpable. Girls who had been brought here from training, moving at the speed of light.

I stop at the door to the basement, where my mother's corpse is surely rotting away. No one had removed her from her cage, and the moment I open the door, the smell has me dipping my head into my shoulder.

The smell hits me like a brick wall as soon as I step into the basement, making me gag. My stomach churns, but I force myself to keep moving. I have to. I make my way to the cage at the far end, the dim light casting eerie shadows on the walls. Two bodies lie inside, twisted and mangled. As I approach, rats scurry away, their tiny claws scratching against the concrete.

I reach the cage door, my hand trembling as I unlock it. The maid, the one who made my life a living hell, lies at my feet. I step over her, my focus solely on my mother. Bending down, I try to reach for her, but the stench overwhelms me. I turn away, clutching the bars as I wretch, my stomach clenching painfully.

When the vomiting finally stops, I take a deep breath, forcing myself to hold it. I grab my mother's arms and drag her from the cage. Her face, her body—she's unrecognizable. I pull her out to the middle of the floor, my hands shaking. Gently, I arrange her arms across her chest, just like they did for my brother in his coffin. The memory pierces through me, the pain of losing both my brothers tearing me apart.

A scream builds inside me, raw and primal, and I let it out. I'm crying, howling, the agony consuming me. Nothing can fix this. Nothing.

The smell of smoke reaches my nose, snapping me back to the present. I'm running out of time. I look down at my mother, my vision blurred with tears.

"I'll see you again in the next life," I whisper, my voice breaking.

I turn and leave the basement, the weight of loss and desperation heavy on my shoulders.

I take slow, deliberate steps out of the building. Each step feels like a weight lifting off my shoulders. The windows are starting to glow, the fire spreading rapidly between the rooms, engulfing everything in its path. My mother's body burns in that mess, burning, disintegrating, wiping out the past.

Makeup ruined, dress askew, I stand outside and watch the fire consume the building. Flames lick the night sky, the heat intense against my skin. The women and girls—now as free as me—gather around. Their faces are a mix of fear and wonder, their eyes reflecting the dancing flames. The night is cold, but this fire, this destructive, purifying fire, is the warmest, most comforting thing we've ever felt.

We stand there, a silent circle of witnesses to our own liberation. The brothel, the symbol of our suffering, burns down, and with it, the ghosts of our pasts. For the first time in a long time, there is a glimmer of hope.

CHAPTER TWENTY-SEVEN

Diarmuid

Watching Niamh is terrifying. She's surrounded by the best people possible, but that does little to calm my nerves. As we dock, a helicopter waits, ready to airlift her to my home, where a team of doctors will be standing by. I want to return with her and Selene, but Victor has requested that I follow him back to St. Gertrude's Church. I know I should leave immediately, but I can't tear myself away until both women are safely on the helicopter.

The crowd watches as Niamh is carried, wrapped in foil and blankets. Her lips are an alarming shade of blue, and her skin looks deathly pale. Selene has been crying, but now she stands strong, clutching Niamh's hand.

"I'll get back as soon as I can," I promise Selene. Her wild eyes and trembling hands make my stomach churn.

"You need to see a doctor, too. Where are you going?" she asks, but it's a question I can't answer.

"I'm fine," I reassure her. "Don't leave her side." I make Selene promise.

I press a kiss to Niamh's forehead and another to Selene's lips before stepping out of the helicopter and signaling for it to take off. The rotor blades churn the air into frantic bursts, and everyone watching clutches their hats and pearls as loose debris and dust swirl around like an angry god's fury.

Slipping out my phone, I make a call to my security team.

"Double the security. Don't let the girls out of your sight," I say firmly into the phone.

"On it," comes the swift reply before I hang up.

With a dip of my head, I slide into the idling limo. As soon as I settle into the back seat, I let my head sink against the headrest, trying to assess the damage to my body. My hands are a bloody mess; my left hand has some flesh missing and won't stop bleeding. My face aches, but it's nothing compared to the ache in my heart when I saw Niamh going overboard. At least she's safe now.

The limo pulls away smoothly, but my mind is anything but calm. I can't help but wonder how safe I am. This whole ordeal has shaken me to the core. My thoughts drift back to the moment Niamh fell, and a shiver runs down my spine. I close my eyes, taking a deep breath, trying to push the haunting images away.

My body feels heavy; the exhaustion from the past hours is

catching up with me. I flex my hands, wincing at the pain. Blood oozes from the torn skin, and I know I need medical attention, but that can wait. For now, I need to get to St. Gertrude's and find out what Victor wants.

Niamh's pale face and Selene's tear-streaked cheeks flash before me. The responsibility of their safety weighs heavily on my shoulders. I can't afford to let my guard down, not now. The thought of them in danger is unbearable.

As the city blurs past the tinted windows, I focus on my breathing, trying to calm my racing heart. How did we get here? And, more importantly, how do I ensure we never end up in this situation again?

Wolf is dead, and that gives me some relief. He can't hurt anyone I love again. The thought brings a bitter sense of solace. But then, my mind drifts to Amira and her damaged face. In the frantic departure from the ship, I hadn't seen her. I know she picked Wolf, but she's still my responsibility. If I survive this meeting with Victor, I will search for her.

I stare out the window, the cityscape flashing by in a blur of lights and shadows. Wolf's demise should feel like a victory, but it's hollow. The scars he left, both physical and emotional, run deep. I clench my fists, ignoring the pain, and think of Amira. Her betrayal stings, but it doesn't diminish my sense of duty towards her.

"Driver, how far to St. Gertrude's?" I ask, my voice sounding weary even to my own ears.

"About ten minutes, sir," comes the reply.

Ten minutes. Just enough time to gather my thoughts and brace myself for whatever Victor has in store. My hands throb with every heartbeat, a reminder of the violence that seems to shadow my steps. I reach for a first-aid kit stashed under the seat, managing to wrap my left hand in gauze. It's a temporary fix, but it'll have to do for now.

I close my eyes and see Niamh's pale face again, Selene's strong yet tearful gaze. They need me to be strong. I can't afford to fall apart now. Wolf is gone, but the ripples of his actions are far from over. There's still so much to fix, so much to protect.

As the limo nears the church, I take a deep breath, steeling myself. I will face Victor, I will ensure Niamh and Selene are safe, and then I will find Amira. One step at a time, I remind myself— one battle at a time.

The limo slows to a stop, and I glance out the window at the imposing facade of St. Gertrude's. This is it. Time to face whatever comes next.

I drag myself up the steps of St. Gertrude's church, every part of my body screaming in protest. The fight with Wolf had taken more out of me than any other fight of my life. My muscles ache, my bones feel brittle, and even my mind is clouded with fatigue. Wolf wasn't human anymore—too far gone, lost to the abyss that every man in our world stares into. It would be so easy to fall, to let the darkness swallow me whole. But I can't. I've always had a reason to stay on the edge, to fight against the pull of the abyss. Especially now, with people depending on me.

I push open the heavy wooden door and step into the cool,

dim interior of the church. The silence here is almost oppressive, broken only by the faint echoes of my footsteps. The scent of old wood and incense fills the air, a stark contrast to the stench of blood and sweat that clings to me.

When I reach Victor's office, I'm surprised to find it empty. The great wooden desk that usually groans under the weight of paperwork and ledgers is completely clear. No papers to pry into, no hints at the webs Victor spins to control the people around him. Just emptiness.

Except for one thing.

On the desk sits an ornate cross, its surface intricately carved and inlaid with gold. The blood of Christ, painted in vivid red, stands out starkly against the pale wood. I know what it means. It's a summons, a call to action that I can't ignore.

A part of me that I haven't faced in a long time stirs uneasily within me. The boy I used to be—the one who trusted the wrong people, who was betrayed by every adult in his life—whispers frantically for me to give in, to let myself fall into that pit. I hate that boy. He's weak, scared, and always looking for someone to save him.

No. I won't be that boy again. I've come too far, fought too hard to be dragged back into that darkness. I have people relying on me now. I have a reason to fight, a reason to stay on the edge.

As I walk past the pews, I can't help but glance at the great statue of St. Gertrude behind the altar. The patron saint of justice gazes down at me with a motherly expression, her eyes filled with a tenderness I've never known. In her hand, she holds a golden cup, and on her chest, a vibrant red, radiant heart pulses with an almost ethereal glow. It feels as if she's silently offering me strength, a reminder of what I'm fighting for.

I slide into the doorway behind the statue, leaving the quiet sanctity of the church for a more foreboding place. The room is long but not too wide, lined with armed men standing in solemn silence. They don't look at me, their gazes fixed ahead, their expressions unreadable. At the head of the room stands Victor.

Age has not diminished the aura of power that surrounds him. Even after all these years, the obedience he's beaten into me forces me to approach him with respect. His cold eyes watch me intently, cruelly, as if dissecting every part of my being.

"Diarmuid," Victor begins, his voice a low, dangerous rumble, "thank you for saving my life."

If only he knew how close that came to not happening. *Amira...* The thought of her makes my chest tighten, but I push it aside. This is not the time.

Victor's gaze never wavers as he continues, "The head of the O'Sullivan family has been chosen, and it is you. Ronan will continue with his business, Lorcan with his politics. But you, my Diarmuid, will be my Warrior King. Now, you are officially the head of an army."

Warrior King. The title is both a burden and a curse, but I remain silent. Victor pauses, clearly expecting some expression of gratitude from me. He receives only silence.

He narrows his eyes slightly but then continues. "Of course, your slate needs to be cleaned."

Victor's words hang in the air, heavy with meaning. He knows why I killed Andrew O'Sullivan. He made me into the deliverer of vengeance, and my uncle was owed that service. But this is different.

Victor's gaze sharpens, and his voice hardens. "It is important to remember that I am the one who commands you."

The weight of his words presses down on me, but I stand firm. The boy I used to be, the one who trusted too easily, would have crumbled under this pressure. But I am no longer that boy. I am Diarmuid, and I have a reason to fight.

Victor's eyes narrow as he watches me. He's been noticing things, picking up on my hesitation when I was ordered to take out Wolf. He knows I haven't been as obedient as he crafted me to be.

"I am ready to forgive you of your sins, of course," Victor says, his voice a low growl. "But you must first pay for them."

He steps aside, revealing a small table that was hidden behind him. On its surface sits a simple, thick candle. Its presence is almost ominous in its simplicity.

Victor's gaze remains fixed on me, searching for a reaction. He finds none. I force my face to remain impassive, my inner turmoil buried deep where he can't reach.

Slowly, I roll up my sleeves, exposing the damaged flesh of my hands. The one I choose to use is particularly mangled from the fight with Wolf, though both hands bear the marks of that brutal encounter. The skin is raw and angry, a testament to the fury that drove me to pummel Wolf's face until my bones protested.

I walk past the guards without a glance, my focus on the table and the task at hand. The air feels thick with anticipation as I position myself beside the table.

Victor strikes a match and lights the candle. The flame flickers to life, casting a warm glow that belies the pain it promises. I stare at it, my mind a whirlwind of thoughts and memories. This is my penance, my path to redemption. For a moment, I think of St. Gertrude's statue, her motherly gaze, and the radiant heart on her chest.

Without hesitation, I lower my damaged hand toward the flame. The heat sears my skin, sending sharp bolts of pain shooting up my arm. I grit my teeth, forcing myself to remain still. This pain is nothing compared to what I've endured, nothing compared to the guilt I carry.

Victor watches me intently, his expression inscrutable. This is his test, his way of ensuring my loyalty. But it's also my moment of defiance, a silent vow that no matter how much he tries to break me, I will not fall.

The scent of burning flesh fills the room, and I can hear the faint hiss of my skin meeting the flame. The guards remain silent, their eyes averted, but I know they're watching. They always are.

I hold my hand in the flame until I can't bear it any longer, then pull it back, my breath coming in ragged gasps. The pain is excruciating, but I stand tall, refusing to show weakness.

Victor steps forward, his cold eyes locking onto mine. "Remember, Diarmuid," he says softly, "I am the one who commands you."

Victor watches, his eyes cold and unfeeling. With a deliberate motion, he pulls a whip from his robes and nods to one of the guards. The guard steps forward and roughly rips the back of my shirt open, exposing my skin to the room. I can feel their eyes on me, but I refuse to show any weakness.

The first lash of the whip is like fire across my back. I clamp my hand over my mouth as the whip kisses me again and again, each strike more painful than the last. My hand doesn't move from my mouth, and I do not cry out, even when the warm trickle of blood runs down my back. Victor is only reopening old scars. This pain is familiar. I've endured it before. I'm not Victor's toy anymore.

Each strike brings back memories of past punishments, but I remain silent, resolute. Victor's face twists with effort as he strikes me until he's panting, his breath coming in ragged gasps. Finally, he throws the whip across the room in frustration, and my blood splatters on one of the guards.

Victor steps closer, his eyes boring into mine. For the first time in my life, I see something in his eyes that I never expected—fear.

Victor steps back, his mask of authority slipping slightly. He extinguishes the candle, but the fire within me burns brighter than ever. I roll down my sleeves, covering the fresh burns and the still-bleeding lashes. The pain is a reminder of my resolve, of the strength I've found within myself.

As I turn to leave the room, the guards part to let me pass, their eyes averted. I walk out of St. Gertrude's church with my head held high, every step a mark of defiance against the darkness that seeks to consume me, the pain that threatens to swallow me.

I won't bend. Not today. Not ever.

CHAPTER TWENTY-EIGHT

Selene

I gently hold Niamh's hand, praying that she pulls through. Her skin is so cold, and I can't stop the tremor in my own hands as I clasp hers tighter. "Please, Niamh," I whisper, my voice barely audible over the roar of the helicopter blades above us. "You have to be okay."

The helicopter jerks as it lifts off the ground, the motion jarring me from my thoughts. I glance at the paramedic, who is focused on monitoring Niamh's vitals. The intensity in his eyes is both reassuring and terrifying. I can barely process the noise, the vibrations, the sheer speed at which everything is happening. All I can do is keep holding Niamh's hand and praying.

We finally arrive at the mansion. The moment the helicopter door slides open, chaos erupts. Doctors and nurses swarm us, their voices blending into a cacophony of urgent commands and medical jargon. Security personnel try to keep the area clear, but it feels like we're in the eye of a storm. I'm pulled along, barely able to keep up as they rush Niamh inside.

The security team refuses to leave, insisting on carrying Niamh to the research room. This surprises me. "Why in here?" I ask, worry threading through my voice. This room contains so much important information; letting all the doctors and nurses in seems risky.

"It's the safest room in the house, and Diarmuid's orders," one of the guards replies. His words hit me like a cold wind. Does that mean Diarmuid thinks we're still in danger? My stomach tightens at the thought.

The security team gently lays Niamh on a bed, and two more guards position themselves at the door, their stances rigid and alert. Only one doctor and one nurse are allowed inside, and I watch as they begin their work, their focus immediately on her chest. My hands are shaking, and when I look down at them, disgust curls deep in my belly at the sight of the blood under my nails. Diarmuid's blood, still there even after he had dived into the water. He had bled as he carried Niamh to safety.

I stand in a daze, barely aware of my surroundings. The doctor and nurse finally step away from Niamh, and their expressions are calm. "She's stable and very lucky," the doctor says, his voice a soothing balm to my frayed nerves. "Niamh must be a strong swimmer." A smile breaks through my pain for a brief second.

"She is," I say softly, more to myself than to them. They nod and leave the room, and I sit beside Niamh, holding her hand. The tension in my chest eases slightly, but questions swirl in my mind. Why did Diarmuid think we were in danger? And where is he now?

For now, I push those thoughts away, focusing on the rhythmic rise and fall of Niamh's chest. She's safe, and that's all that matters. I rest my head on the edge of the bed, exhaustion pulling at me, but I refuse to leave her side.

A maid arrives, and she gently urges me to change out of my blood-stained clothes. I don't want to leave Niamh, but I know she's in good hands, if only for a few minutes.

I finally leave Niamh, my steps heavy with exhaustion. The chaos has quieted down, and the house feels eerily calm. I make my way to the bathroom, my body moving on autopilot. Once inside, I strip off my clothes and step into the shower.

The hot water cascades over me, washing away the grime and blood but not the fear. I lean against the wall, and the tears come, unbidden and uncontrollable. I cry for Niamh, for how close I came to losing her. I cry for the shock of what had happened, the terror that still grips my heart. Every sob feels like a release, yet the weight in my chest doesn't lighten.

And then, Diarmuid. Where is he? Is he safe? The worry gnaws at me, even as the water pounds down. He had been so strong, so determined, but he had been hurt. I replay the scenes over and over, my mind refusing to rest.

After what feels like an eternity, I turn off the shower and dry myself off. My reflection in the mirror shows red-rimmed eyes and a face etched with worry. I take a deep breath, trying to steady myself and get dressed. I need to be there for Niamh, and I need to know what's happening with Diarmuid.

I return to Niamh's side, the room still and quiet. She's lying there, breathing steadily. I sit beside her, taking her hand once more. The fear hasn't gone, but being here with her, I find a small measure of peace. I just have to wait now and hope that Diarmuid comes back soon with good news.

The room is quiet now, a stark contrast to the chaos of earlier.

"Diarmuid will be back soon," I tell myself, the words a fragile anchor in the storm of my thoughts. I close my eyes, trying to steady my breathing. All I can do now is wait, and hope that when he arrives, he brings some semblance of good news.

I lie on the bed in the research room, gently petting Niamh's hair; I watch her closely. Her eyes blink slowly, weak but alive. Relief floods through me, knowing she's here, breathing.

"You are so strong, Niamh," I murmur, my fingers tracing patterns through her hair.

"That is what Diarmuid told me," she whispers, her voice barely audible.

"Hm?" I lean in closer, unsure if I heard her right.

"That's the only voice I remember," she continues, her eyes staring into the distance. "Diarmuid's. Telling me how strong I am."

A pang of sadness hits me. "He wouldn't wait for help. He went in immediately after you."

"I am grateful," Niamh says, a faint smile touching her lips.

I squeeze her hand, feeling the fragility in her grip. "Once you're better, we'll arrange for you to see Ella. I'll deal with your parents."

Niamh laughs softly, a sound so delicate it almost breaks my heart. "That won't be necessary anymore."

Her words hang in the air, confusing me. What does she mean? But I can't bring myself to ask. Not now, not when she's like this.

Instead, I hold her hand tighter, offering silent comfort. The mysteries and questions can wait. Right now, all that matters is that Niamh is here with me. Alive and strong.

I hear the door open and instantly hope surges in my heart. Diarmuid steps in, wearing a heavy jacket, and he looks utterly exhausted.

He glances at Niamh, who has finally fallen asleep. "How is she?" he asks, his voice rough with fatigue.

I hold a finger to my lips, gently untangling myself from Niamh. Together, we tiptoe out of the room and head to the master bedroom. I close the door behind us, giving us a moment of privacy.

"How are you?" I ask softly.

Diarmuid's eyes flicker with concern. "How is Niamh?" he counters, ignoring my question.

"She is recovering. She is alive. Thanks to you," I reply, gratefulness filling my voice.

As I watch him, I notice Diarmuid moving stiffly, his movements labored. Worry knots in my stomach. "Let me help you with that," I say, reaching forward to help him take off his jacket. He's too stiff to do it on his own.

The sight that greets me is horrifying. His flesh looks ruined; not a single piece of skin has its regular color. It's all inflamed, and blood is caked in patches.

"Oh, Diarmuid," I breathe, my heart aching. "Victor?"

Diarmuid nods, a grim confirmation.

A surge of anger and sorrow threatens to knock me over, but I hold firm. "We need to get you cleaned up. Sit down," I instruct, trying to keep my voice steady. I can't afford to lose it now.

He sinks onto the edge of the bed, and instead of staring at him in horror, I leave, enter the bathroom, and grab a washcloth, running it under the tap until it's soaked with warm water. My hands are steady, but my heart feels like it's breaking. From under the sink, I retrieve the first aid kit and some fresh towels, bracing myself for what I have to do next.

Diarmuid is still sitting on the bed when I return, the soft glow of the chandelier casting shadows across his back. The sight stops me in my tracks, a lump forming in my throat. His back is a mess of cuts and bruises, and the stark reality of his suffering hits me like a physical blow. Everything about this is so wrong. Did he struggle? Did he fight back? Or did he have to just accept the whipping, like he must have as a child?

Tears run down my cheeks, but I force myself to keep the emotion out of my voice. He's been so strong through all of this, and I need to be strong for him now. "Diarmuid," I say softly, trying to keep my voice steady, "I'm going to clean you up, okay?"

He nods without looking at me, his shoulders tense. I walk over and sit beside him on the bed, carefully dabbing the washcloth against his wounds. The silence between us is heavy, filled with unspoken pain and questions. My hands tremble slightly, but I keep going, gently wiping away the blood and dirt.

"You don't have to do this," he says quietly, his voice rough with fatigue and pain.

"I want to," I reply, my voice firmer than I feel. "You've done so much for us. Let me take care of you now."

He doesn't argue, and I continue my task, each touch a silent promise that I'm here for him. The tears keep falling, but I brush them away quickly, not wanting him to see. He needs strength right now, and I'm determined to give it to him.

As I finish cleaning his wounds and start applying bandages, I steal a glance at his face. The pain etched there is almost too much to bear, but I force myself to keep going. He's always been the strong one, but tonight, I need to be strong for him. I can't help but think of the sacrifices he's made, the pain he's endured for us. The gratitude and love I feel for him are overwhelming.

"We'll make it through this," I whisper, more to myself than to him, determined to heal these wounds, both seen and unseen.

His face, hands, and neck are a bloody mess, and the washcloth is already soaked in blood. I swallow hard, trying to steady myself. "Do you want to shower?" I ask, unsure if something as simple as running water would cause him pain.

Diarmuid looks at me, his eyes weary but resolute. "Yes," he says, his voice hoarse. He rises slowly, every movement clearly causing him discomfort, but he doesn't let it show.

I lead him to the bathroom, turning on the shower and adjusting the temperature. The steam begins to fill the room, and I hope it will be soothing for him. "I'll help you," I say softly, my voice barely above a whisper.

He nods, and I help him undress, my heart aching with every new bruise and cut that's revealed. Once he's in the shower, the water cascades over him, mixing with the blood and washing it away. I stand by, ready to assist, but also giving him the space he needs.

Diarmuid closes his eyes, letting the water run over him, and I can see the tension in his shoulders begin to ease. "How does it feel?" I ask, hoping the water is more comforting than painful.

"Better," he murmurs, his voice softer now. "Thank you, Selene."

I grab a fresh washcloth and gently start cleaning his face and neck, careful to avoid the worst of his injuries. The blood slowly washes away, revealing the raw, angry wounds beneath. "You're so strong," I whisper, more to myself than to him.

When I see the burn on his hand, a sob escapes me. "I want to kill him, Diarmuid," I whisper, the words raw with anger and grief.

He doesn't respond, but his eyes meet mine, and there's a flicker of something—gratitude, perhaps, or relief. I continue to clean him as best I can, my hands steady now, my heart full of a fierce determination to help him through this.

I'm surprised when he cups my face in his hands; his touch is gentle and reassuring. His lips meet mine in a deep, soulful kiss that makes me collapse into his arms.

As I cling to him, a realization hits me. Maybe I need to take a page out of Amira's book and burn all of this to the ground. The thought hardens something within me. Earlier, I had heard the news about what Amira did. Maids gossip and news travels fast. With the fall of Wolf, she seems to have lost her mind, yet I can't help but have some respect for her.

"Let's get you dressed and into bed." I offer Diarmuid.

He nods, but his gaze is fixed on me, and words hang in the air unspoken, words that send my heart skyrocketing. After what feels like an eternity, he follows me out of the steam-filled bathroom. I grab some boxers and leave the rest of him bare. Before he gets in bed, I check the waterproof bandages to make sure they are still intact. They are.

Once he's asleep, I leave Diarmuid resting in bed, his breathing finally even. I head to the research room to check on Niamh one more time before I sleep.

As I enter the room, I'm startled to see Niamh out of bed, moving about frantically. Panic surges through me. "Niamh, you need to rest," I say, rushing to her side, trying to guide her back to bed.

But Niamh grabs me, her eyes wide and almost mad. "Selene, no! You don't understand," she says, her voice a frantic whisper. "I have to... I have to find it..."

"Find what, Niamh? Please, you need to lie down," I plead, my heart racing with fear for her.

She shakes her head vigorously, her grip on my arm tightening. "No, Selene. It's important. I need to find it before it's too late," she insists, her desperation palpable.

I look into her eyes, trying to understand. "Okay, Niamh. We'll find it together. But first, you need to rest. You're still recovering," I say, trying to calm her.

Niamh hesitates, her breath coming in short, uneven gasps. "Promise me, Selene. Promise you'll help me," she demands, her eyes searching mine.

"I promise, Niamh," I say softly, finally managing to ease her back into bed. As she lies down, I stroke her hair, my mind racing with worry and determination. Whatever it is she's searching for, I'll help her find it. We'll find it together, no matter what it takes.

"Do you see it? Do you see him?" Niamh's voice pulls me out of my thoughts, her tone frantic.

I turn to see what has her so agitated. The wall is plastered with photos of Sophia Hughes at various events. But it's not Sophia who's circled in red ink—it's someone else. In each photo, a person in the crowd is marked. My eyes widen as I recognize the face that appears repeatedly.

Michael.

Diarmuid had educated us about the hierarchy of the hands of kings that he knew, and I remember Michael was important to Victor—a Page, but Victor's Page.

Niamh's voice trembles with urgency. "Do you know what this means?"

My heart sinks as realization hits me. "Sophia Hughes must

have been a Bride to Michael before he was stripped of his title," I whisper, the weight of the truth settling over me like a heavy shroud.

Niamh nods, her eyes wide with a mix of fear and revelation. "He was always there, always watching. We focused so much on Tyrone and Sophia that we missed the real threat."

Michael. How could we have been so blind? My mind races, piecing together the implications. If Michael was there, then he would have been involved in everything. The attacks, the manipulations—it all ties back to him.

"Selene, what do we do?" Niamh asks, her voice shaking.

"We need to regroup," I say, my voice firm despite the dread curling in my stomach. "We have to find out everything we can about Michael and his connection to Sophia. And we need to do it fast."

Niamh's eyes search mine, desperate for reassurance. "We can't do this alone."

"We won't," I assure her, squeezing her hand. "Diarmuid, Amira, everyone—we'll all work together. We'll take him down."

As I help Niamh back into bed, my mind is already strategizing. This revelation changes everything. We need to act quickly, decisively. For Niamh, for Diarmuid, for all of us.

I leave the research room, my heart heavy with the knowledge of what we're up against. But beneath the fear, a steely resolve takes root. We will uncover Michael's plans, expose him, and put an end to this nightmare.

Back in the master bedroom, I find Diarmuid resting. His

presence is a balm to my frayed nerves. I want to climb in beside him but decide to leave him and return to Niamh.

As I close my eyes, I know that tomorrow brings a new battle. But for now, I draw strength from the warmth of his body next to mine, the promise of our shared fight giving me the courage to face whatever comes next.

I can't sleep. The sheets are tangled around me, a physical manifestation of my restless mind. Niamh's chest rises and falls in a dream-filled sleep. I hope she's having better dreams than I am. I was back on the yacht watching her go overboard. I decide to creep downstairs, hoping a glass of milk might help. As I tiptoe down the stairs, the house is eerily quiet. Usually, the soft hum of the security and the occasional creak of the old mansion accompany my nocturnal wanderings. Not tonight.

The lights in the hallway are out, casting deep shadows that stretch like fingers across the floor. I pause on the stairs, my skin prickling with unease. Something tells me to turn back, but I push the thought away. Just nerves, I tell myself—just nerves.

Movement ahead draws a sigh of relief from me. It must be one of the security men doing his rounds. I step off the stairs and into the hallway, my foot bumping into something soft. Confused, I kneel down, my fingers brushing against a familiar uniform. A gasp escapes my lips as I realize it's one of the security men, his neck twisted at an unnatural angle.

My heart thumps wildly in my chest, a drumbeat of terror. I open my mouth to scream, but a gloved hand clamps over it, stifling the sound. I'm yanked backward, dragged toward the front door. Panic surges through me, every instinct screaming for me to fight, to escape.

But the grip is ironclad, and my mind is a whirlwind of fear and confusion. What's happening? Why is this happening? I struggle, my thoughts a desperate litany of questions with no answers.

CHAPTER TWENTY-NINE

Diarmuid

I wake up, my heart pounding, my dreams still echoing with the terror of my childhood. The twisted faces of Victor and Andrew, their voices taunting as they melted my skin, jar me into consciousness. For a moment, I'm paralyzed, the lingering fear making me think I'm back in that hellish training camp. I can almost hear the crack of the whip, feel the searing pain in my back. I wince as the memory becomes too vivid, a phantom pain flaring where the lash had struck.

I glance to my left, expecting to see Selene's reassuring presence, but the bed is empty. A cold sense of dread creeps over me as my fingers reach out, touching the cold, undisturbed spot where she usually lies. "She must be with Niamh," I mutter to myself, trying to shake off the unease.

With a groan, I force myself out of bed, every muscle protesting as I move. The memory of the whipping feels too real, and I can almost hear Victor's sadistic laugh. I leave the room, the hallway dimly lit, and make my way to the research room, where I told security to place Niamh. The sight of her asleep, alone, does little to calm my nerves. There's no sign of Selene. Panic begins to bubble up, but I push it down, forcing myself to think clearly.

I rub my eyes, exhaustion settling deep in my bones. The agony that Victor inflicted on me blends with the fatigue, making each step heavier than the last. As I turn to leave, the photos on the wall catch my attention. Fresh red circles highlight one person in each picture. "Michael." My heart pounds, a cold realization settling over me. When had the girls made this discovery? The implications are staggering. Michael, the one person who seemed untouchable and unsuspected, is now the prime suspect.

As I step back into the hallway, every sense is heightened. The silence is oppressive, like the calm before a storm. I begin to race down the stairs, each step echoing in the quiet. "Selene!" My voice reverberates, but there's no answer. The silence feels wrong, ominous. I pause on the final step, shapes on the floor catching my eye. My breath hitches, and I tiptoe to a long sideboard, reaching underneath. My fingers brush against the cold steel of my weapon, a reassuring touch in the midst of chaos.

I walk cautiously to the first dark shape on the ground. It's one of the security guards, lying still. I check for a pulse, but he's dead. Panic surges, but I clamp down on it. Someone's in the house. I can't call Selene's name again; I can't give away my position. Moving through the house, I find more bodies, each one sending a fresh wave of dread through me. After a full sweep of the bottom floor, I turn on the lights, illuminating the carnage. The house is a tomb.

Then it hits me—Selene is gone. The realization crashes over me like a wave. Someone took her. My mind races, piecing together the fragments of the night. The red circles around Michael's face in the photos. The dead security guards. It all points to one horrifying conclusion.

Michael.

I grit my teeth, a surge of determination pushing through the fear. I will find Selene. I will stop Michael. But first, I need to gather my wits, my strength. The fight is just beginning.

I try to steady my breathing, but the dread is almost suffocating. Each step I take feels heavier; the shadows in the house seem to stretch and twist with malice. My mind races back to the training days, the cruel drills, the endless hours of torture designed to break us. I survived that, I remind myself, trying to muster some courage. But the thought of Selene, somewhere out there, alone and possibly in danger, makes my stomach churn.

As I move through the house, I grip my weapon tighter, ready for any sudden movement. The silence is deafening, broken only by the sound of my ragged breaths. I check each room meticulously, my eyes scanning for any signs of a struggle, any clue that might tell me where Selene is.

In the living room, I find more security guards, their lifeless bodies sprawled across the floor. Each one is a grim reminder of the danger lurking in the shadows. I kneel beside one, checking for any signs of life, but it's clear they're all gone. Who could have done this? And why? My mind circles back to Michael. The images on the wall, the red circles…they haunt me. What did he want with Selene?

A sudden noise from upstairs snaps me back to the present. My heart leaps into my throat as I slowly ascend the staircase, each step measured, silent. The upper floor is darker, the shadows deeper. I strain my ears, trying to catch any hint of movement, any sound that might betray Michael's presence. I reach the top of the stairs, the hallway stretching out before me like a dark tunnel.

I move from room to room, the dread growing with each empty space. My mind is a whirlwind of fear and anger. I picture Selene's face, her smile, the way she used to look at me with such trust. I can't fail her. Not now. Not ever.

Down the hall, the research room beckons. I approach slowly, the darkened door a sliver of doom. I don't want to peer inside, and yet, I can't get there fast enough. There's something there I need to see— I reach the door and lift haunted eyes to Niamh's bed.

Empty.

I enter the research room, but Niamh's bed is empty. I spin and race back down the hallway silently.

I reach the last door, a heavy wooden barrier at the end of the hall. My hand shakes as I grip the handle, pushing it open slowly.

Niamh screams. When she sees me, she finishes pulling up her trousers. "You scared me."

Her gaze falls to the gun in her hand. "Diarmuid?" Fear fills her voice, and she shakes her head, walking toward me. "Diarmuid, what is it?"

I lower the gun, knowing the house is empty. "It's Selene. She's been taken."

FIND OUT WHAT HAPPENS NEXT IN

WHEN KINGS FALL

OTHER BOOKS BY VI CARTER

THE CELLS OF KALASHOV

THE COLLECTOR #1

THE SIXTH #2

THE HANDLER #3

MURPHY'S MAFIA MADE MEN

SINNER'S VOW #1

SAVAGE MARRIAGE #2

SCANDALOUS PLEDGE #3

SONS OF THE MAFIA

SINS OF THE MAFIA #0.5

VENGEANCE IN BLOOD # 1

YOUNG IRISH REBELS SERIES

MAFIA PRINCE #1

MAFIA KING #2

MAFIA GAMES #3

MAFIA BOSS #4

MAFIA SECRETS #5

WILD IRISH SERIES
FATHER (PREQUEL)
VICIOUS #1
RECKLESS #2
RUTHLESS #3
FEARLESS #4
HEARTLESS #5

THE BOYNE CLUB
DARK #1
DARKER # 2
DARKEST #3
PITCH BLACK #4

THE OBSESSED DUET
A DEADLY OBSESSION #1
A CRUEL CONFESSION #2

BROKEN PEOPLE DUET
DECIEVE ME #1
SAVE ME #2

ABOUT THE AUTHOR

Vi Carter - the queen of **DARK ROMANCE**, the mistress of suspense, and the high priestess of *PLOT TWISTS!*
When she's not busy crafting tales of the **MAFIA** that'll leave you on the edge of your seat, you can find her baking up a storm, exploring the gorgeous Irish countryside, or spending time with her three little girls.
Vi's Young Irish Rebels series has been praised by readers and can be found in English, Dutch, German, Audible and soon will be available in French.
And let's not forget her two greatest loves: *coffee and chocolate.* If you ever need to bribe her, just offer up a mug of coffee and a slab of chocolate, and she'll be putty in your hands.
So, if you're ready to join Vi on a wild journey with the mafia, sign up for her newsletter and score a free book! Just be warned - her stories are so **ADDICTIVE**, you might not be able to put them down.

WHAT READERS ARE SAYING

Editorial Reviews

"Vi Carter has once again blown my mind with another outstanding story. She never fails to create a masterpiece with memorable characters that leap off the page. This book is complete perfection."- USA Today Bestselling Author Khardine Gray

Vi is one of those authors who never disappoints. She weaves LOVE & DANGER effortlessly. *5 stars!*

I definitely recommend this book. It is SUSPENSEFUL and exciting. I enjoy reading Vi Carter's book. *5 stars!*

HOW TO KEEP IN TOUCH WITH VI CARTER

Visit Vi's website: https://author-vicarter.com/.

Join the newsletter: t.ly/yZWbX

Or scan the code below:

On Facebook, Instagram, TikTok and YouTube @ darkauthorvicarter and on Twitter @authorvicarter

Or scan the code below:

ACKNOWLEDGEMENTS

I'm very lucky to have such amazing readers and Beta Readers. I want to thank the following people who worked with me on this book.

Developmental Editor: Lori Wray White

Proofreader: Sherry Schafer

Blurb was written by: S.R. Frederick

Formatter: Elise Hoffman

Co-plotter: S. R. Frederick

https://pen-nibblers.com/about/

Beta Readers:

Lucy Korth

Tami Thomason